HOCKEY MOM

A Romantic Suspense Novel

EVE LANGLAIS

Killer Moms # 2- A Bad Boy Inc. Spin-off

PROLOGUE

THE POLICE REPORT stated that it appeared as if his snowmobile went through the ice. The tracks ended at the edge of a hole that dropped into the chilly, deep lake. It being the end of the freezing winter season, Antoine should have known better than to ride across the cracking ice.

But her boyfriend, like many other boys his age, enjoyed the thrill. After all, Antoine wasn't even twenty yet. Too young to die.

His death proved a sobering experience.

Devastated, Tanya cried for days. Skipped school, too, and hung out at their place in the woods. Not much of a hangout. An old tree fort abandoned years ago by whoever had built it, but it became their spot. They met there in secret because his parents were strict when it came to girls.

"You can't come over, my mom will kill me." As to

spending time at her house? Also, not happening. Her parents were assholes. Especially her dad.

The treehouse didn't have a bed, only a plywood floor, but Antoine got them a blowup air mattress and a blanket. Which worked great during the warm days of summer and the coolness of fall, not so much fun in the winter. Yet Antoine did his best to ensure that she never shivered with cold when she was with him—only pleasure.

Given that they both belonged to the geekiest club in school—the one that got to use the computer lab—they often stayed after the others had gone, locking the classroom door and making love by the glow of a screen.

Why did he have to die? To think, they'd only been months away from graduating and being able to leave this shithole. His words, not hers. The town itself was fine. A little boring and judge-y, but no worse than anywhere else.

"Where will we live?" she'd asked more than once when he told her of his plans.

"I'll find a place."

Antoine never doubted for a moment that he'd escape. She didn't think he ever imagined it would only happen in death, however.

She mourned his loss and became determined to fulfill his dream. To leave this place and never look back. In between going to school, she got a job and began squirreling away all her money. A mere pittance that trickled to nothing the day her boss caught her puking in the back and asked if she was pregnant.

How long had it been since her last period?

Too long as it turned out, and her grief at losing Antoine turned to joy. A part of him lived inside her.

Excited, she announced it to her parents.

Who stared at her. Her mom's head began to shake. "Why would you go and do that?"

As for her dad... "Are you fucking kidding me? I don't think so. We were just about to get rid of you. Don't expect us to start paying for a bastard."

"What are you saying?" Tanya expected them to freak out when she told them about the pregnancy, maybe even demand an abortion—which she'd refuse. But she assumed--very wrongly—that they'd ultimately support her.

Tanya didn't expect them to toss her out. That wasn't supposed to happen. They gave her five minutes to pack her shit.

"Why are you doing this?" she cried as she stuffed clothes into her bag.

"Bad enough I raised your mother's bastard. I am not raising someone else's."

The words stopped her dead. She looked at her father, big and mean, then at her mother beside him. The parent she'd gotten all her looks from. But she'd always wondered about her brain.

It made so much sense now.

Tanya slung the backpack over her shoulder,

shaking inside with fear, but only because of the unknown.

As the door slammed shut behind her, part of her was tempted to whip around and pound on the solid wood panel. Maybe kick it a few times.

Instead, she headed for the road, muttering, "You know what, I don't need you."

She didn't need her no-good family. Her father with his quick temper, her mother with the sharp slaps. Even her brother, who thought it was okay to take pics of her in the shower to sell to his buddies.

She could make it on her own. She spent too much of her savings on a bus ticket out of town, but she couldn't stay here. She also couldn't afford to rent a room. Not if she wanted to eat.

Hitting a library, she used their internet capability to locate an address for a women's shelter. The people working there proved kind, if pushy, especially once they found out about her *situation*. Because, yeah, announcing that you were pregnant got all kinds of tones, whispers, and knowing expressions as they said, "Parents were pro-lifers, eh?"

Their faces when Tanya told them that it was she who wanted to keep the baby? A strange mixture of shock and then condemnation. Because they believed she'd made the wrong choice, they took it upon themselves to subtly pressure her. The number of abortion pamphlets pushed into her hands made her grind her teeth. As her belly swelled, and that option became unavailable, the adoption hints started.

"...*a family who can give your child the life they deserve.*"

"*Think of those poor couples who can't have a baby of their own.*"

None of them understood that Tanya would never abandon the life growing in her belly, the only connection she had left to its father.

When the loneliness got to be too much, she stroked her hand over her swelling abdomen. She might have lost her boyfriend to a freak accident, but a part of him lived on.

Unfortunately, the shelter provided only a temporary respite. Not to mention, the people there were driving her nuts. Tanya chose to move out rather than wonder if they'd go so far as to rip her baby from her when it was born.

While in the shelter, she'd saved up some money, enough for first and last month's rent. Or a laptop.

The computer won, meaning, she had no place to live, a situation she resolved by squatting in empty homes. Amazing how many people went away on holiday once the weather got cold. So easy to get inside.

It kept her off the streets as she entered the last weeks of her pregnancy. Once the baby came, she'd let the hospital care for her, milking it for as long as she could. Thank you, free Canadian healthcare system.

Except the hospital didn't keep her very long, the

curse of being healthy. By the time she left with her baby boy—perfect in every way—she'd found her next place to squat. Finding empty homes to live in proved easier than expected once you got into the right social network neighborhood groups.

I need someone to pick up my mail while I'm gone.

Dog sitter required while I'm at work.

So many places she could borrow for a few hours here—eating out of their fridge—a few nights there—sleeping in a real bed with the baby snuggled against her side.

It never bothered her that she stole, not when it meant caring for the baby boy who owned her heart.

Since leaving him with a sitter wasn't an option, Tanya hacked for extra money. It was the one skill she had that only required a computer and an internet connection.

Holding websites for ransom? That paid a nice chunk. Blackmail over dirty pictures, and even a little bit of online shopping with stolen credit cards. Nothing huge. And never the same place twice.

Still, as careful as she tried to be, it ended up drawing attention. Not with the cops, though. She would have known since she monitored them.

Tanya never even knew they were coming. They just appeared in the condo she'd appropriated—the owner some kind of interior designer out of town on business—guns outstretched, expressions grim, all women.

Which she found intriguing.

The one who appeared in charge of them possessed smooth, ebony skin, high cheekbones, and an appraising gaze. "You're not what I expected to find."

"I'm sorry. I'll pay for the food I ate and leave."

"How did you get in?" the woman asked.

Clutching her baby boy, terrified and hoping they'd take pity, Tanya hung her head and said, "I picked the lock."

"No, you didn't." The woman holstered her gun and crossed her arms. "You took over the condo's security system, including the door lock mechanism. You looped the cameras to make it appear as if no one was here."

"How did you know?"

"You're in Ontario. Every house has a smart meter, so imagine my surprise when I got a ping saying that my usage was higher than normal."

"This is your place?" Tanya's heart sank, and as if sensing her agitation, Cory began to fuss.

"Yes."

"What are you going to do with me?"

"Given you broke through the best security system available out there?" The woman she'd later know as Marie Cadeaux smiled. "Offer you a job, of course."

CHAPTER ONE

THE AIR WAS CRISP, sharp enough to bite the lungs, and especially knife-like when huffing and puffing for dear life. The muscles in Tanya's thighs burned as she pushed to keep out of his reach.

Her stride was long, the blade of her skates catching the hard ice and shaving it. Push, glide, lunge. She held her upper body partially hunched, making herself smaller and offering less resistance to the wind.

It didn't matter. She could hear him getting closer. The *schwick* of his skates eating up the ice louder and louder.

She put on a burst of speed. Adrenaline coursed, awakening all of her muscles. Faster, she had to go faster. He couldn't catch her.

Movement at the side caught her attention. She turned to look and...saw her cheeky son sail past, not even breathing hard. Waving and smiling.

The show-off circled back to do laps around Tanya as she slowed. Out of gas, she came to a halt and leaned over, hands on her burning thighs, trying to breathe without dying.

Being in shape from working out inside a gym couldn't compare to being on skates outside in a cold snap that could literally freeze body parts in minutes. A good Canadian girl, she knew how to dress, but she couldn't bundle her lungs.

"You did pretty good that time," her son teased.

Little jerk. He'd even given her a head start. She just about burst with pride at his athletic ability.

"Put me on a treadmill, and I'll show you who's slow." She was better at paced endurance competitions.

"Treadmills are for hamsters," sassed her son, the comedian.

"And full dishwashers are for mouthy brats." A rebuke said with a smile.

He would have emptied it no matter what. Cory had always been good about his chores, but she worried about the rest of his teen years. Wasn't this when the rebellion started? Another parent had mentioned that she'd caught her son with a vape. Some new method of smoking. Gross.

Cory would never do that. Would he? Tanya eyed him as they slowly skated back towards their car and the treat of the day: freshly deep-fried Beavertails!

Nothing like the sight of tourists' eyes widening

with horror when Canucks teased about eating the delicacy. Their clear repugnance never failed to amuse. They honestly thought people meant meat. Ugh. As if.

The real stuff was a fluffy pastry, deep fried to crisp, golden perfection, and then, if going for the original and basic flavor, sprinkled with icing sugar. Or, you could go a little crazier: apple and caramel drizzle, Nutella and banana, even cheesecake was possible.

Cory went for the chocolatiest thing they had on the menu, all the better to get it all over his face and hands. Casting glances at him as they drove from the canal that ran down the middle of Ottawa, Tanya was happy to see the boy still lurking in there. There was time enough later for him to be a man.

Christmas lights twinkled as darkness fell early upon the city, the days now at their shortest. Winter had arrived early this year in Ottawa, bringing with it record cold. The sub-Arctic temperatures were the only reason the canal opened so early. December twenty-seventh, only midway through Cory's school holidays, and the day before his hockey tournament in Mont Tremblant, Quebec. It wasn't too far of a drive, but they would be staying overnight.

Tanya had already packed for the trip: snow gear, comfy clothes, warm jammies, extra clothes for Cory—because his packing skills usually involved one extra shirt and a toothbrush—and his snowboarding equipment. The hockey bag was ready to go, and she already had her kit in the back of her SUV under the spare.

Because what hockey mom ever went anywhere without her gleaming Magnum and other toys? Never knew when you'd need some explosives or some rappelling rope.

When Cory went to bed that night, she signed on to her workplace website via a secure terminal. The dancing flower jiggled the moment she plugged the hidden flash drive into the USB. Someone in the Killer Moms office had a sense of humor when it came to hiding technology in plain sight. Immediately upon logging in, her inbox showed three messages.

The first... *Schedule recap: Wedding rehearsal on Wednesday. Wedding on Friday.* The group chat response: *What's on Thursday?* Carla's pre-wedding jitters bride reply was: *Getting drunk.*

Tanya grinned. That sounded like Carla. Who would have ever thought she'd get married? Hell, no one ever thought she'd retire, and yet the legend that was Carla—the one with the most kills under her belt and an almost perfect record when it came to mission completion—had already left the Killer Moms agency, KM for short, to work for her newly discovered grand-dad. Turned out, she had family apart from her son. She'd even fallen for a guy during her discovery of her new grandfather. Most mind-blowing of all? She was happy.

Which, if you knew the grouchy Carla, was a pretty amazing thing. Her wedding would be epic. Since it was happening on a beach during the March school break, it meant that Tanya should think of upgrading her old bathing suit from her mom one-piece to maybe a tankini.

Maybe.

She wasn't looking to draw attention. Didn't need a man in her life. She had her son.

Tapping a reply on her keyboard, Tanya sought to reassure the nervous bride-to-be. *Can't wait. This is going to be great.*

Sappy, but that was Tanya. She loved the idea of her friends, who'd all suffered hardships, finding a happily ever after.

Perhaps it's time I thought about dating, too.

The girls had a point when they teased Tanya about not being with a man for over a decade. Actually, it was closer to fifteen years. Heck, Antoine was barely more than a boy when they were in love, and he'd left her with a gift that ensured she'd never forget him.

Rest in peace. Dead so young, her chance at happiness ripped away in a freak snowmobile accident.

But at least he lived on in Cory.

Tanya moved to the next email from Mother, the code name used for her handler with KM. *Tell Cory I'll give him a hundred dollars if he manages a hat trick.*

Shaking her head, Tanya smiled as she tapped a reply. *Better have it ready.* Because her son played extra hard for treats. Knowing that, she'd had to change his reward from a donut per point to five dollars. She should have started lower. It was costing her a fortune.

13

The last message was more of a warning.

Careful on your trip.

Tanya doubted she'd run into trouble. The tournament was for pleasure, not work. Mostly. She planned to test a new software program she'd written and hoped to use in the field.

Shutting down her computer, she spent some time doing last-minute checks. Luggage packed. Doors and windows locked. Son sent to bed with permission to socialize for half an hour online.

At eleven o'clock, she sat on the couch with a glass of white wine for a moment of relaxation. It lasted all of three minutes. Then, the screaming next door started.

Which was fine. People fought. It was the thumping, then the sudden silence that made her tense. Especially since she knew what it meant.

A black eye. Maybe an arm in a sling. Feeble excuses, blaming clumsiness. And Tanya had reached the limits of her patience. It was past time she did something.

Dressing in dark clothes, Tanya grabbed a bottle of water and went into the shared back yard. The row of townhouses had only one big fence around the shared yard. Her salted steps and grippy boots meant that she kept her footing as she descended and then stuck to the shadows behind the houses. Her nose wrinkled as she stepped on the discarded cigarette butts lying all around. The abusive neighbor liked to litter.

The water she poured immediately frosted on the cold surface, the bare spots on the poorly shoveled stairs greedily grabbing it, making them treacherous. Which was perfect. Only one asshole tended to use these steps.

She went to bed and managed to sleep until dawn when the screaming started again. She was brushing her teeth by the time the flashing lights appeared on the street out front.

Cory glanced at them with curiosity. "Did Mrs. Lewinsky have another accident?"

"Not this time, buddy." This time, Mr. Lewinsky, one drink too many in his system, went out for a smoke and took a fatal header off the back stairs he didn't like to clear.

Couldn't happen to a nicer man.

CHAPTER TWO

THE DRIVE to Mont Tremblant proved uneventful. Not one moose ran across the road, to Cory's disappointment. He had the camera on her phone ready just in case. The boy had this crazy desire to capture the video of all videos. He claimed if he went viral, they could be rich.

"Money's not everything," she replied. Besides, they had more than enough stashed in an offshore account. Not that her son knew about Mommy's *other* job. He, like everyone else in her mundane life, knew Tanya as the interior designer for KM, a prestigious company with ties around the world.

"If we were rich, I'd have a cell phone like my friends."

"You're only fourteen. You don't need a phone." A battle she clung to, despite knowing he had a point. But she wasn't ready to give in yet.

His lower lip jutted fiercely. "You're treating me like a baby. Everyone has one."

"If everyone jumped off a bridge, would you?" she countered.

"Depends. How high is the bridge?"

She cast him a glance. "You do know the correct answer is: 'No, Mom, jumping off a bridge is a dumb and dangerous idea.'"

He grinned. "I think that's the point, Mom."

"Don't you dare," she admonished as she turned into the parking lot of the hotel. Having arrived a day early, they'd have a chance to unwind and check out the slopes. At least, Cory would. Tanya would be sipping hot cocoa by the gallon while doing her best to hack a few of the guests' computers for fun.

"You going to let me ride something other than the baby hills this year?" Cory asked.

Her first impulse as a mother was to scream, "*Never!*" Instead, she used the one trick that would work with Cory. "Why don't we see what your coach says."

"Why have a tournament in Mont Tremblant and have us stay at the lodge if we're not going to snowboard?" Cory rolled his eyes. "And I know exactly what Coach will say." He deepened his voice. "Better not break anything. We got a big game tomorrow."

She bit her lip lest she laugh. Cory sounded just like Coach Bryan. "I never said you couldn't snowboard. But I don't know if you're ready to hit those really steep runs."

"I am a pro, Mom."

"I know you are, Skee." The nickname fashioned after the great one, which she'd given Cory not long after he clutched his first hockey stick in his chubby hand. He'd lived up to Gretzky's rep. Perhaps not with as many goals because Cory played defense, but as an all-around star asset to his team.

"Please, Mom." The begging came with a dangerous set of adorable, brown eyes.

Saying yes meant relinquishing yet another part of him, admitting that he was grown up. Tanya hated it. She sighed. "Fine. But if you get hurt—"

"You'll freak out and overreact. I know." The sighed reply was accompanied by an eye roll.

It tugged at her lips. Little jerk. But her little jerk. "Love you, Skee."

"Mom!"

"What?" She blinked with pretend innocence.

"Someone might hear you," he hissed.

"Hear what? Me saying I love my amazing son." She might have shouted it.

He slouched down. "Seriously, Mom?" He slunk from the car, and she kept grinning. Okay, so there were parts of the teenage thing that could be entertaining.

The ski resort had two options for guests: tiny chalets with gas fireplaces and rustic charm, or the lodge itself, with a dining room and one massive living room for guests, replete with a giant stone fireplace that always had flames licking behind the black metal screen.

Since trudging through snow for breakfast didn't appeal, Tanya chose the lodge. It had better Wi-Fi.

With her son being at the age where privacy for them both became paramount, she'd gotten a one-bedroom suite, which meant a bedroom with a door, and in the larger living area, a pullout couch with a mini kitchenette.

"Mine." Cory called the couch, and she didn't even think of arguing. Kids had the oddest ideas of what was fun. Sleeping on lumpy springs wasn't one of them in her book.

It didn't take long to unpack. Cory unzipped his bag and was piling on snowboard gear, ready to go.

She didn't rush to join him. He already had his slope pass, so she told him to go ahead without her to the intermediate hill, which was a slight concession.

She began her drill of precautions. "No talking to strangers. No leaving the marked trails. Don't fall off the lift. Nothing stupid or fancy. Be back in time for lunch."

He sighed. "Anything else to ruin my fun?"

She grabbed his cheeks and rubbed his nose with hers. "Don't get hurt."

"Geez, Mom. You trying to jinx me?"

"Fine. Break a leg."

"Will do," he crowed, running out the door.

Her turn to sigh. No fear. None at all, just like his father. At times, that frightened her because look what had happened to Antoine.

Only when she'd locked the door behind him did she truly unpack.

The false bottom in her suitcase came out. The specialized router that would mask her signal got plugged into her battered laptop—to anyone peeking, it looked like a simple USB memory stick.

A set of keystrokes that never appeared on screen logged her into the program she'd designed. She liked to call it Big Sister is Watching. If it worked as she hoped, then this would probably go down as some of her finest work—and when her handler sold it, it would add yet more zeros to her bank account.

The first thing the program did was catalogue all the signals in the lodge. Hundreds of them. Cell phones, laptops, other routers, even a thermostat, she noticed as she kept an eye on the scrolling list.

Once the list was compiled, a subroutine would launch and begin attaching files to each device. If the signal belonged to a person, it would include their name and a dossier of everything known about them that could be found online. Even objects would get processed. The whole deal would take hours.

If it worked. This would be a heavy-duty test, given how many people were moving in and out of the immediate area.

Letting it run meant that Tanya had time to check and see how Cory was doing.

She arrived at the bottom of the hill wearing a knitted cap, scarf, and thick, wooly mittens. The sun might be shining, but the air remained crisp. Every breath fogged.

Shading her eyes and glancing uphill, Cory was easy to spot, his lime green suit vivid at the top of the awfully steep mountain. "And that's supposed to be intermediate?" she mumbled.

Cory pushed off and zipped down, going way too fast. It made a mother's heart stutter.

A heart that stopped as he hit a bump and soared. Arms out, legs tucked, the board attached to his boots flipping at his command. He landed in a slight crouch and began picking up more speed, heading for another hump in the slope. Hitting it, he went airborne, legs canting to the side, high enough he slapped his boots before landing again.

By the time he swooshed at the bottom, spraying her legs and feet with snow, she was clapping.

"Mom! Mom! How'd I look?" he asked eagerly.

Being a mother, she had to tease. "Not bad. Although you could have tucked your legs a little tighter on the third one."

"And here I thought he was excellent."

A frown pulled at her brow at the familiar voice. An impossible voice. She whirled, and her jaw dropped as she saw him.

Looking almost the same as the last time she'd seen him.

Just as handsome.

And alive.

"You!" Before she could think twice about it, she shoved Devon, ex-colleague and asshole, into a snowbank.

CHAPTER THREE

"MOM!" Her son sounded so shocked.

Sitting in the cold snow, Devon wasn't. "Hey, Bunny. Long time no see." He used the old nickname from the job they'd done together.

"Not long enough," she muttered, looking adorably grumpy.

Her boy eyeballed them before asking, "Do you know this guy, Mom?"

Intentionally yanking her chain, Devon grinned. "You might say we're old friends."

"Friends is pushing it." Tanya crossed her arms. "What are you doing here?"

"Skiing and admiring the view." Which stood over him with arms crossed. It was the most fun he'd had in a while. "You?"

Her gaze narrowed in suspicion. "Cory is in a hockey tournament."

"Ah, so you're the reason barely a room can be found. I had to settle for a tiny cabin. The last one down that path." He pointed.

"I'm sure they'd make room for you in the kennel if you're not happy."

Devon almost laughed, not because of the insult, but because of the look on her boy's face. A boy who listened just a bit too avidly, making it hard for Devon to say much.

Ignoring Devon, Cory turned to his mom. "I'm starved. When can we go eat?"

Rising from the snowbank, Devon brushed himself off before shoving a hand into his pocket and yanking out a twenty, which he dangled in front of Cory. "Why don't you grab yourself something while I chat with your mom."

The kid didn't touch it and eyed him suspiciously. "Mom says to never take money from strangers."

"Name is Devon." He held out his free hand. "Nice to meet you."

Hesitating for only a second, Cory thrust out his own palm, and they shook, a simple, firm grasp with the kid testing his strength. Devon knew better than to try anything fancy with the handshake. Last time he'd done that with one of Harry's kids, ending in a pretend gun and wink, the whole family had practically died of amusement. Cool uncle Devon he was not.

"I'm Cory."

"And now we're no longer strangers." Devon

twitched the twenty once more at the boy.

"Why do you want to talk to my mom alone?" the kid asked instead of grabbing the cash.

If this were someone older, Devon would have fucked with him and said something wildly inappropriate, but this was a kid. One who was eyeing and appraising him boldly. "Er, because I need, um..." He wracked his brain for her job. Hoped he got it right. "Decorating tips."

"You want to hire her?" The kid's nose wrinkled. "I still don't get why people do that. Paint your walls a color you like. Buy comfy furniture." The roll of the eyes eloquently spoke of what Cory thought of his mom's interior design career.

It was hard not to smile, especially given that Bunny frowned. "Be glad I talked you out of painting your room that god-awful orange."

"Would have been epic," the boy defended.

"It would have hurt your eyes. Go grab something hot to drink, and some fries or something."

Bunny snatched the twenty and shoved it at her boy.

Cory grabbed it. "How long you gonna be?" The boy spoke to his mom but eyed Devon.

"Just a few minutes," Bunny said.

Devon put a hand on his heart. "I promise I won't keep her long."

"But—"

"I'll be fine. I can handle Devon." She smiled as

Cory finally gave in to the starvation of his teen stomach and slouched off towards the lodge.

"Good-looking boy."

"Yup."

"How old is he?"

"Why do you care?"

"Because you hardly seem old enough to have a child that age."

"I look good for my age."

She looked damned good. Devon pegged her for late-twenties, early thirties maybe. And as feisty as ever. At least, with him. For some reason, she had a chip on her shoulder when it came to Devon.

During their last—and only—mission, he hadn't gotten the sweet smiles and laughter the other operatives enjoyed. Even their room service fellow got a nicer hello than Devon did.

"How have you been?" he asked.

"What are you doing here, Devon? Because knowing you, it's probably not good."

"Me?" He pretended aggrievement. "Just making polite conversation."

"Since when are you polite?"

"Bunny, I am tickled you remember me," he exclaimed.

"As if I'd forget," she muttered darkly. "You and that stunt you pulled on that job."

"That was years ago, back when I was a lot rasher."

"Rash? Why don't you try suicidal?"

"I survived."

"Barely."

"I'm touched you were worried about me."

"Worried your agency would blame me for your death. That was a stupid move you pulled that almost got you killed."

"It worked, though." He grinned. He and his fake wife, Bunny, had infiltrated a bank that was laundering money. While he created a sizeable distraction, she'd downloaded the information needed to prove the bank's illegal activities. "Our mission was a huge success." And even though they'd shared a room together as part of their cover, they hadn't celebrated in bed. Back then, Devon had an obligation waiting back home.

Funny how people always assumed he was a lady killer, the kind of man who screwed anything that winked at him. And he was—when single. When part of a couple, he took his role as lover seriously. A pity his fiancée hadn't.

"I have to say, given your propensity for breaking rules, I'm surprised to see you still around."

"Like a cat, I always land on my feet."

"Or you're close to running out of lives," Bunny retorted dryly.

"Would you care if I died?" Would anyone give a damn when he was gone? A question he'd been wondering of late.

"Care?" She arched a light-colored eyebrow. "Not

really, unless you're doing some fool stunt that tries to take me with you."

"I'm a changed man, Bunny."

"Who still insists on using that ridiculous nickname." She pressed her lips into an angry line, looking cuter than a bunny, all soft and cuddly.

"Would you prefer sweetheart?"

"I'd like it if you used my name."

"You mean the one you never gave me? All I ever knew was your fake persona. Marie-Josee Poirier. What is your real name?"

Rather than reply, she said, "Enough with the small talk. What are you doing here?"

"Enjoying some epic skiing. Gorgeous slopes here. And I hear the restaurant makes a mean prime rib dinner."

Her lips pinched. "You are so full of poop, your eyes are brown."

"Hazel."

"Don't make me drop your butt into the snow again."

"Bunny, if you want to touch me, you don't have to ask." He flirted. Outrageously. Mostly because the high color in her cheeks made him ridiculously happy.

"You are lucky people are watching, or I'd shoot you."

"You're lucky there are people watching, or I'd kiss you," he confided.

Which earned him an, "Oooh, you are so bad."

"Yes. Yes, I am." He took pride in his finer points.

"What are you really doing here? And don't feed me another line about skiing."

Devon rolled his shoulders. "Why do you think I'm here?"

"You've got a job."

"Maybe. You really here for hockey?"

Her head bobbed. "And the hot cocoa. Did you know they serve it with full-sized marshmallows?"

The very cuteness of it went well with her actual appearance. Petite blonde, hair shoulder-length, porcelain skin pink from the cold. Body hard to tell with the layers over it, but he recalled it being trim. Not that he'd done anything about it six years ago. At the time, he was engaged. That didn't work out.

Eyeing her hands hidden in gloves, he wondered if she sported a ring. "You bring the hubby, too?" He wasn't big on subtlety.

"Still not married. Not looking. And not interested."

"Shot down, and I wasn't even trying. I think I might be offended."

She snorted. "No, you're not."

A grin pulled at his lips. "When does your boy play? I might pop by the arena." It still surprised him that she had a teenage son. Then again, the secret agency she worked for didn't call itself Killer Moms for nothing. They only recruited single mothers down on their luck.

"Cory has three games starting Friday."

"So, what's the plan for this afternoon?" Not sure why he asked, especially since he wasn't supposed to get distracted.

"Relax and read while Cory hits the slopes."

"Want to hook up for dinner?" The moment the words left his lips, he almost slapped himself. She'd made it obvious what she thought of him. She'd never say yes. But then again, a man had to try. Look at how she stuck around to chat. Why, her very body language screamed, "*interested.*"

"No, thanks."

He blinked. "Why not?" Again, not what he meant to say.

"I don't date."

His first impulse was to clarify that it wasn't a date, but... "Why don't you date? Bad breakup?" Had she sworn off men?

He expected her to bullshit him. Instead, he got the naked truth. "I was in love once. With Cory's dad. He died, and it just doesn't seem right to hook up with anyone else."

"You mean you've been single..." Knowing approximately how old the kid was meant the math was... "...a long time." The idea baffled. She was a gorgeous, young woman. Surely, she didn't plan to stay single forever?

"It's okay. I've got Cory. Speaking of whom, I should go check on him." She went to walk past Devon.

He managed to say, "Nice seeing you again, Bunny."

The raised middle finger brought a chuckle. Yup, still sporting a chip on her shoulder when it came to him. And it wasn't just because of the mission. Six years ago, she'd hated him on sight. It didn't help that they'd had to share a room. Not that anything ever happened. She kept firmly to her side of the bed. Got dressed and undressed in the bathroom. The most intimate they got was sharing the sink to brush their teeth so they wouldn't be late for their mission.

Devon still remembered how their eyes had met in the mirror. They'd both paused in brushing. Stared... And then he spat out the foam in his mouth and made a show of rinsing. He'd been attracted to her six years ago, but he'd never acted on it.

Did she sense it? Was that why she disliked him?

Staring at the lodge she'd disappeared into, Devon had to wonder if Bunny was telling the truth about being here because of a hockey tournament. Technically, he had no reason to doubt her. No reason to trust her either. Which might have been why he forgot all about skiing and pulled out his phone.

The number he dialed was answered by the receptionist, Sherry, with a perky, "You've reached Bad Boy, Inc., the only realtors who can make all your property dreams come true."

"Hey, Sherry."

"Devon, why are you calling the office? Aren't you on vacation?" she chided.

"Totally. About to hit the slopes. But, funny thing, I ran into an old Canadian friend of yours. The interior designer I met years ago on my trip to Vancouver. But felt like such a dweeb. I couldn't remember her name."

No need to say more. With her almost photographic memory, Sherry knew exactly who he meant, even though he'd been working for the west coast branch at the time. "Goodness, what a small world. How is Tanya?"

"Looking great. Her son is in a hockey tournament and, wouldn't you know, they're staying at the same resort. Such a small world."

Except the world wasn't that small, and for two operatives to end up in the same place...

Sherry exclaimed, "Isn't that a coincidence. Or, maybe it's fate. After all, you're both single. You should totally ask her out to dinner."

"I did."

When he said nothing further, Sherry snickered. "Holy smokes, our resident Casanova got shot down. Poor, Devon."

It wasn't funny. His ego felt rather bruised. Which might be why he said, "She's not interested in guys because she's pining for her kid's dad."

"But he's been dead almost fifteen years," Sherry said.

"Yup." What else could he say? It boggled the

mind.

Sherry laughed. "I can't believe you bought that excuse."

"What?" It had never even occurred to him that Tanya might have lied. She seemed so sincere.

"You know, I haven't talked to her mother in ages. I think I'll give her a shout. I'm sure she'd get a kick out of hearing you bumped into each other again." That was code for Sherry would look into seeing if Tanya was here on personal business or a Killer Moms job.

"See you next week in the office." He hung up and pondered the mystery of Tanya fabricating a story about remaining faithful to her one true love to deflect Devon's interest.

Except, the joke was on her. He found her more intriguing than ever. He headed for the lodge, deciding to do lunch before he went skiing. Maybe he'd get another peek at her.

She didn't seem like she was here on a mission, and if she were, no way she'd bring her kid. Then again, it would make a great cover.

It was also crazy dangerous. The guys Devon was supposed to watch out for weren't choir boys. So, if they did show up, he should probably warn Tanya. According to his source, they were scheduled to arrive mid to late afternoon, which meant, he had time to work on his cover of a guy here to have fun.

Now, if only that fun involved a bed, a naked Bunny, and marshmallow fluff...

CHAPTER FOUR

SO MUCH FOR having a fun afternoon. An alert had appeared on Tanya's phone during lunch, which meant that she'd possibly be cancelling her massage.

The warning indicated that Big Sister is Watching, the program she'd left processing, had run into a snag. Of course, it would happen during lunch, right when she'd finally—after a long wait, due to the kitchen being busy—gotten her club sandwich and crispy fries. She eyed the layers in her sandwich with the perfectly toasted bread, the green edges of the lettuce peeking, the hint of red tomato, and the juicy, grilled chicken breast. Add to that the bacon and garlic aioli, and it became mouthwatering.

Her phone blinked at her, reminding her that she needed to reset the program. And she would, after she finished her lunch.

Biting into her toasted oral orgasm, she listened as

Cory babbled, his speech rapid-fire and animated. Just not with her. God forbid he actually talk to her in public.

His gradual withdrawal over the past few months since he'd begun ninth grade, hurt. The only consolation was the fact that at least he didn't act like Tanya had the plague when they were alone. But out in public? As *the mom*, she was relegated to watching and listening as Cory chattered with another boy who'd also arrived early. The pair were determined to get some serious snowboarding done before hockey the next day.

With someone his age to hang with, Cory inhaled his food and was off with a quick, "Later, Mom."

Watching him saunter off, his face animated, and his mouth open wide in laughter at something the other kid said, Tanya couldn't help but miss the days when he used to hold her hand everywhere they went. During his younger years, she used to hate leaving him to go on missions. When she absolutely had to travel, one of the KM aunts—comprised of older, retired assassins who took on more protective roles—watched over Cory.

She'd not needed a sitter in a while. Nowadays, Tanya did most of her work from home. Only in rare cases did she travel for the KM office that acted as a legitimate business front for her hacking duties—specialized missions that mostly involved espionage, her ability to hack into systems without compare.

Mother had known what she was doing when she recruited the squatter in her condo almost fourteen years ago. Going to work for Mother—Tanya's handler and mentor—had saved her and Cory. Gave them a stable home, a new kind of family. Plus, a job that paid big bucks. Given that Tanya owed KM everything and hated when stuff went wrong, she cancelled her massage and returned to her room. Upon seeing the error message on her laptop screen, she did the simplest thing first. She stopped and restarted the program.

Unable to detect any signals.

Impossible. The place should be flooded with them. She pulled out the USB device and blew on it. Checked inside for dust. Reinstalled and then tried again.

Unable to detect any signals.

When the basics failed, it was time to reboot. Tanya did a soft restart of the computer—Error!—followed by a hard reboot. The program refused to find any signals, but of more interest was the fact that even her phone couldn't detect anything. No cell phones or even the public Wi-Fi the hotel offered.

More and more curious.

Exiting her room, she rode the elevator downstairs to a hum of excited voices, all complaining about the same thing: lack of service and connectivity to use their phones and smart devices.

Immediately, her mind went to Devon.

He had to be behind this. Never mind the fact that Tanya had no proof. He would have access to this kind of technology. The question being, did he jam the signal from his little cabin? Or did he plant the jamming device somewhere more central?

There was only one way to find out. Usually, she would have hacked the reservation database for his room information. With the internet down, she'd have to resort to more hands-on methods like questioning the people manning the front desk. However, that might have to wait given it buzzed with irate people demanding access to a working phone.

Heading outside, the brisk air made her breath catch, and she noted the sun dipping in the west as the afternoon waned. She'd spent more time than expected working on the stubborn signal problem. Cory would be returning by suppertime when darkness fell. She had to get this fixed before then.

The paths to the tiny cabins were well indicated and clear, but she didn't have to go far before her phone suddenly beeped, flooding her with messages.

It appeared the signal returned once she got a certain distance from the lodge. That didn't stop her from marching the rest of the way to Devon's cabin and rapping sharply on the door.

No answer. For a moment, Tanya thought about busting in, but the fact that her signal worked outdoors probably meant he'd hidden the jamming device somewhere inside the main lodge.

With purpose in her step, she marched back to the building, sighing at the daunting prospect of searching the lodge for what might be a very tiny device. She needed a way to pinpoint exactly where it was located. It would require her to program a subroutine—something some people would have bitched and moan about —however, Tanya loved a challenge.

She returned to her room and went to work, her legs tucked lotus-style with her laptop in her lap. Her fingers flew over the keys, and her eyes remained focused on the streaming characters across the screen. The code took shape, the instructions set via values and expressions, subroutines of those results easy to perceive. She never understood those who called it gibberish.

As soon as she had a prototype, albeit a rough one that might prove glitchy, she loaded the new app onto her phone. The code ran and changed how her smartphone looked for a signal. Her screen pinged with a pulsing dot. She walked towards the door of her room, and the dot remained steady. As she took the elevator down, the dot suddenly flashed quicker for a second, then slowed again. A glitch, or something else?

Hitting the main level, Tanya noted the increased crush of people as night fell and skiers returned from the slopes, bringing with them the crispness of the outdoors but at the same time, the warm and wet heat from so many bodies and melting snow.

She lifted herself up on tiptoe, looking for Cory in

the crush. He proved easy to spot, his bright green coat unzipped. He hung with a gaggle of boys, which meant he wouldn't welcome her intrusion, which was fine. She could use a few more minutes to work on the signal problem.

Angling her phone, she watched the screen. The signal appeared faint on this side of the room and weakened the closer she got to the door leading outside. About to turn around and search in the opposite direction, the door opened, sending forth a blast of cold air. A frisson went over her skin, and she glanced up from her phone screen to see Devon, hair rumpled, cheeks red. Tanya quickly turned away.

What was it about this man that frazzled her? Six years ago, she'd felt just as flustered. He warmed her in places that had no right getting hot. He teased and flirted outrageously. Yet not once did he take anything further.

Which should have pleased, but it disappointed. And Tanya hated Devon for making her so confused.

It seemed that hadn't changed. One peek at him, and arousal simmered. Best to not look.

Now's my chance to ask him if he's the one jamming the signals. Perhaps that was part of his mission.

Or maybe it wasn't Devon at all, but something more devious.

Whatever the case, Tanya needed the jamming to cease. Eyes on her screen, she noticed the pulsing dot quicken as she crossed the room and headed for the stairwell rather than the elevator.

Not too many chose to use the stairs after a day of skiing, especially past the second floor. By the time she'd sprinted up the first flight, she was alone, thumping along the steps made of black metal grates, the appearance at odds with the homey decor in the main rooms.

As she neared the third level, the pulse on her phone flashed rapidly. Almost there.

Below her, a sudden clamor erupted when the door opened, and someone entered the stairwell. Rather than looking down, she kept skipping, the heartbeat on her phone pulsing faster.

Just around the next turn, the third level, she burst onto the landing and glanced around, at first seeing nothing but beige walls and a closed grey door with a metal handle across it. Here, or a little higher? Going up to the next level slowed the seeking dot.

Back to the third, then. This time, she really looked around. It took mere seconds to spot the flash of light.

Tanya dropped to her knees and looked under the riser. A tiny, red light blinked. She reached for it and plucked the electronic culprit free. It didn't take much to crush the device and render it inoperable.

Take that, Devon!

She was feeling pretty smug until a deep voice startled her. "What are you doing?"

CHAPTER FIVE

WHEN DEVON RETURNED from an afternoon of skiing, he decided to hit the lodge for a hot drink instead of his cabin. The fact that he might catch a peek of Bunny had never once entered into that decision. Which might have been a lie given how he checked out every single blonde he spotted.

Entering the main building, he heard a hum from the people milling around, a good number of them holding up their phones and exclaiming.

"...shit freaking signal."

"That's it. I'm changing carriers when I get home."

It seemed more than a few phones were on the fritz, including his he noticed when he glanced at the screen. Not completely unheard of. Some buildings skewed signals more than others. But it was odd, considering that it hadn't occurred earlier.

More than likely, something had happened to the

cellular tower for this area. Given the issue was wide-spread, Devon would wager it wouldn't take long to fix.

Unzipping his coat to combat the humid warmth of the room, he scanned the space, noting and dismissing the majority of its occupants. The flash of a green coat thrown over a couch drew his gaze to Cory hanging with some other kids his age, but no mom sat beside him.

Glancing past the boys, Devon spotted Tanya only by accident when some bodies moved, giving him a clear shot. She pivoted, phone in hand, a slight frown between her eyes. The sweater she wore was a big, comfortable, woolly thing. Her leggings molded to her legs, but he couldn't see past mid-thigh given the length of her top.

She appeared to be ignoring the noise around her. Could be she was reading something interesting on her phone. Or on the hunt for something.

She walked briskly towards the stairs, and he couldn't help but follow.

What are you up to, Bunny? Did she have something to do with the signal issue?

Entering the stairwell, he paused and listened. Heard the steady thump of someone going up ahead of him.

Please don't let it be too many stories. His legs ached from skiing. It only took one flight for them to start burning in protest. A guy his age—past the mid-thirties mark—needed to take it easier on his body.

Never. Devon didn't want to get old, so he gritted his teeth and kept climbing until he rounded the corner of the third level and saw Bunny standing there, looking at something in the palm of her hand.

"What are you doing?" he asked.

For a second, she startled, and her hand dropped to her hip. "You!"

"Someone's a little jumpy."

"Don't sneak up on me," she said with a scowl.

"Hardly sneaking given you could hear me coming. What have you got there?" Devon asked, noticing she'd curled her fingers around something.

"Why don't you tell me?" She held out a chunk of plastic.

It didn't take much to decipher what he saw. "Ah, the signal jammer."

"So it is yours!" She shook it at him.

"No."

"But you just admitted to knowing what it is."

"Process of deduction. My phone stopped working the moment I entered the lodge. And then all of a sudden, it was fine again."

"How can you tell?"

His lips curved. "It's giving me good vibrations."

"That's gross."

"Only if you put it somewhere it can get stuck."

She sighed. "You're impossible to talk to."

"Yet you're managing just fine. How did you find the device?" Devon asked.

"I created an algorithm that reversed the usual interpretation of signals and instead sought the absence of them."

He blinked at her. "In English, please?"

"An app to find the doohickey."

"Putting your hacker skills to work," he said with an approving smile. "I'm surprised you'd bother given you're on vacation. Shouldn't you want to unplug?"

She pursed her lips. "I can't download a book to read without a connection."

"The gift shop has paperbacks you could have bought."

"Are you arguing with the fact I located the device and nullified it?"

"No, I'm just pointing out the holes in your logic. Like Swiss cheese, Bunny."

She crossed her arms. "Why are you here? I thought you were staying in a cabin."

"I am."

"Yet, here you are."

"I am. I blame you. Ever since you told me the hot cocoa has big marshmallows in it, I've been craving some."

"I'm not stopping you. Go." She shooed him.

"Leave when this is much more interesting?"

"Is this related to your mission?" She shook the device between two fingers.

He shrugged. "What mission?"

At her glare, he smiled.

"Seriously, I have no idea who it belongs to." The truth.

Her lips pursed. "But it could belong to the person you're after. What's their name?"

"Now, Bunny, you know I can't answer that." He grinned.

"You will because I've got my son here with me, and I won't have him put in danger if you're involved in a mission that might go violently awry."

"Would it help if I said violence isn't expected?"

"So, you admit you're here for work!" Her *aha* tone of voice made him roll his eyes.

"Duh. I mean, think of it, why would I come to Canada to ski when Denver is closer?"

"What's your mission?"

"Mission, what mission?"

"Don't make me drain your bank accounts and have a warrant put out for your arrest," she threatened.

The corners of his eyes crinkled as he laughed. "Geezus, you don't mess around."

"Tell me what you're up to."

"Only if you have dinner with me." Apparently, he had masochistic tendencies.

"Excuse me?"

"You want me to spill my guts, then the price is a meal with me."

Her gaze narrowed in suspicion. "What's the catch?"

45

"No catch. No sex. Unless you're interested." He arched a hopeful brow.

"Not even if it would save your life."

He winced. "Ouch, Bunny. That's harsh."

"Best to get that out in the open. It helps with any misunderstandings later."

"And here I was just trying to be friendly. You want info, then the price is dinner with me. As friends," he quickly added.

She still found a reason to refuse. "I need to eat with Cory."

"You mean the boy who is hanging with a gaggle on the main floor, currently demolishing several boxes of pizza?"

Her lips drew into a flat line. "He's a teenager. He'll need more than a few slices."

"You're right. Give him a few dollars, and I'm sure he'll manage to scrounge up more food. Or does he need his mommy to cut it for him?" Yeah, he was a bit of a dick, but it was her fault for hating him so much. Something he'd yet to understand. She acted as if he'd wronged her.

"You're bossy," she stated.

"Then say no. I don't care. But don't expect me to tell you anything."

The door behind her suddenly opened, slamming into her body and shoving her into Devon, who had only a second to glimpse a large, looming shape coming through.

Instinct—and a whole lot of desire—had him slanting his mouth over hers, capturing that soft, pink cupid's bow.

It was supposed to be a kiss to cover their presence in the landing, but the heat of it captured him. Aroused him. Especially since she kissed him back!

At least for a second before she pulled away, her cheeks flushed and her eyes bright. "Devon!" she exclaimed.

"Sorry, Bunny. Looks like someone caught us." He smoothly tucked her into his side so that he might better face the big fellow glowering at them.

"What are you doing here?" grumbled the guy dressed in a parka, his brows thick and dark, his head quite bald in contrast to his goatee.

"Trying to convince my honey bunny that it's not too early to go to bed." Devon winked.

"Devon!" She squealed his name again and turned, her hands between their bodies, hiding the device she'd found.

Was this guy a simple guest, or had someone noticed that the jammer had stopped working?

"Move," the goateed guy ordered.

"Sure, buddy. Sorry. Didn't mean to get in your way. After you, Bunny dear." He spun her and gave her a swat on the butt. She jumped and squealed, then took one step towards the stairs and managed to stumble.

"Ouch. Oh, my foot." She bent down, and Devon

could have groaned at the sight of her ass rising up, the sweater falling away enough to show off the round curve. He wasn't the only one staring at her butt. The guy who'd interrupted them almost got a shot to the face because of it.

When she straightened, she scowled. "Some kid left a toy on the stairs, and I stepped on it. I could have really hurt myself."

"Kids these days have no respect." Devon plucked the debris from her hands, pretended to give it a cursory glance, and then tossed it in a corner. "How about I kiss your booboos all better?" He gave her another smack on the ass, and she glared at him before giggling and racing up the stairs. Devon chased after her.

He listened for signs of pursuit but heard nothing. On the fourth floor, he signaled for her to be quiet, then grabbed the door. He opened then shut it hard.

They stood there in silence. It was faint, but they heard muttering. "Clumsy fucking blonde. Boss is gonna be pissed."

Bunny's eyes widened. Devon put his finger to his lips, and they waited to hear the clang of a door before Devon opened the one on the fourth floor again and slipped through, quietly latching the portal behind them.

Only when they reached the far end of the hall, did Tanya whisper, "He knew about the device."

"Yup."

"You know the guy?"

He shook his head. "Nope."

"Are you lying to me?"

He couldn't help but grin. "Have dinner with me, and you can find out."

"Fine. I'll meet you in the dining room at eight p.m."

"Really?" He couldn't help but sound surprised.

"Yes, really. Don't worry. I'm already regretting it," she muttered before stomping off toward the elevators.

He didn't follow. No need to antagonize her further. It wouldn't take much to change her mind, and knowing Bunny as he did, she'd look for any reason to cancel, which was why he needed a backup plan.

CHAPTER SIX

TANYA COULDN'T BELIEVE she'd agreed. Having dinner with Devon was the worst idea, especially given that her lips still tingled from that impromptu kiss on the stairs.

When she stumbled into him, she couldn't help but note his strength, his scent, and then the heat when his mouth sought hers.

A kiss shouldn't have the ability to so thoroughly arouse. Yet, Tanya couldn't deny the lingering tingle in her lips. The ache between her legs. The anticipation of seeing him again.

Which was why she wouldn't go. Making it to her room, she instead concentrated on restarting her program, wondering if that rude fellow had another jammer to use. Although she didn't understand why he'd put it in a stairwell.

Why not keep it in his room? Then again, he may

have counted on the metal of the stairs acting as an antenna to push his signal farther.

Who was the guy? Was he Devon's target? She had no idea. The fellow was obviously up to no good, and she believed this even though she knew nothing about him yet. To investigate the big, rude jerk, she required a name at the very least. Even better would be a phone number so she could filch information. She could even work with a digital picture. But all she had was the brief glimpse she'd gotten of the guy's face.

Didn't matter. Tanya had come on hockey mom business, not work, and with the signals feeding her Big Sister program, she would eventually find out. Thus far, the information she retrieved hadn't raised any flags—even without a mission, she and the other operatives kept an eye open for possible terrorism and other major crimes. Despite nothing popping out, all of the info gleaned on this trip would be stored in a secure database. You could never own too much information.

With the jamming device disabled, the Big Sister program began humming along again, leaving Tanya with nothing to do. Just in time for Cory to come barging into the room, his arms full of damp gear that he promptly dumped in a pile on the floor.

"Seriously?" she asked with an arched brow.

"You're such a mom," he grumbled, grabbing his stuff and at least draping it over the backs of chairs.

"Did you have fun?"

"Yeah."

"Did you eat?"

"Yeah."

"Did someone cut out your tongue?"

Cory stuck it out and then laughed. "Had pizza with the guys in the lobby. Saw your buddy, Devon."

"Oh, what was he doing?"

"Taking off. The valet dude brought him a car, and he left like half an hour ago."

"Good for him. I hope he has fun." Did that mean he didn't plan to meet her at eight? She'd never find out because she wasn't leaving this room. "How about you and I splurge and order a movie on the pay-per-view channel?" she suggested, indicating the television.

"Me and the guys were planning to hang out."

"Oh." Did she look as crestfallen as she sounded?

For a moment, he looked torn. Obviously not liking his mom's sadness, but at the same time being a teenage boy who didn't want to hang out with his mother.

A knock at the door saved them. Before she could holler at him to stay away from the door, Cory had moved to answer it. She shifted closer to the dresser drawer that held her gun. It was the safest place she could hide it, considering that Cory wouldn't think of putting his clothes away. When they went to tournaments, he lived out of his suitcase.

"What do you want?" was Cory's rude greeting to the man at the door.

"Cory!" she exclaimed.

A seemingly unoffended Devon grinned. "Hey,

big man, I brought some food. Hungry?" Devon dangled a paper bag that looked suspiciously like Chinese.

Her favorite.

Cory sniffed. "I smell eggrolls."

"And lemon chicken, crystal beef, pork fried rice, and chow mein."

Her stomach rumbled. "Sorry, you went to the trouble. Cory was just leaving to meet his friends."

"Then that means more for the two of us." Devon winked.

"Maybe I should stay." Her boy glanced from Devon to her.

For a second, her son's protectiveness warmed her motherly heart. But having Cory as a buffer meant that Devon couldn't talk freely. And since she suddenly found herself curious again...

"Don't worry about your old mom. Go and have fun." She waved at the door.

Cory didn't budge. "On second thought, maybe I should get to bed early. You know, get lots of rest for the games tomorrow."

"Hey, if you stick around, you can help me choose colors." Devon fished into his coat pocket and pulled out some paint cards. "I'm stuck between dove gray and Arctic gray. But I wonder if maybe I should go wild and choose the ever-classic heather gray."

The boredom and panic set in quickly. "You know what, I really should go and say hi to the guys. Just for a little while. I'll be back before ten," Cory promised before sliding out the door.

Devon shut the panel behind her son and then faced her, looking much too attractive and oddly awkward as he said, "Hey."

"What are you doing here?"

"I thought we agreed on dinner."

"In a restaurant." With people. Lots of people in public where she wouldn't be thinking of the bed only feet away.

"Please, we both know chatting openly would have been impossible. And I hear they're running almost ninety minutes to get food."

Her nose wrinkled. "Some of their waitstaff is sick, so they're short-handed."

"Hence why I popped out and grabbed us this." He shook the bag, and she sighed as she gave in less than gracefully.

"Fine. Let me clear a spot." She snared her laptop from the table, the screen saver an image of Cory in full hockey gear a few years ago, his grin somewhat gap-toothed.

Devon started laying the food on the table, and the smells enticed. Tanya sat down across from him and eyed the various plastic dishes and the distinct lack of plates and utensils.

"Um, Devon, I think we have a problem."

The corners of his eyes crinkled. "Guess we're going to have to eat old school." And then he demonstrated by snaring a piece of chicken, dipping it in the lemon sauce, and eating it. With his fingers.

"I'd like to see you do that with rice."

He solved that problem by raiding her coffee stash. As with most hotels, there were wooden stirrers, that he used as impromptu chopsticks.

Eyeballing the ease with which he used them, she thought, *great idea*. Until she tried it and ended up losing all but one grain of rice.

She stared mournfully at the pile she'd dropped on the table.

"Let me help, Bunny." Before she could protest, he'd snared the sticks and brought a portion of the rice to her mouth. She had no choice but to eat.

It was delicious. Or so Tanya assumed. She didn't really taste much given that she was more intrigued by the man sitting so close to her.

He'd stripped off his coat and laid it over the couch, leaving him clad in only a snug, long-sleeved t-shirt tucked into his jeans. The incredible physique she'd admired six years ago was still there.

"How often do you work out?" she asked, only to realize how it sounded.

"Whenever I can. You?"

Her nose wrinkled. "I make myself go to the gym five days a week."

"Make?"

A moue contorted her lips. "I'm not big on the whole exercise thing. It's boring."

EVE LANGLAIS

"Then you're not doing it right."

"Don't tell me you're one of those guys who likes getting sweaty and pumped?"

He laughed. "I do like the adrenaline rush, but it's easy to exercise by incorporating it into your daily life. For example, I tend to take the stairs instead of the elevator. Walk instead of drive, if I can."

"Which is great cardio and good for the legs. What about the arms?"

"Pushups and crunches while listening to the news every morning before my shower."

"Before my shower, all I want is coffee," she commented. They might have flirted and shared pleas-antries all evening, except her computer beeped.

It drew both of their gazes.

"Not here on a job, huh?" he said, picking up a piece of beef.

"An interior designer's work is never done."

That caused him to snort. "Nice try. What are you snooping for?"

"Nothing. What about you?"

"Nothing." He held her stare.

"You said if I had dinner with you, you'd explain what you're up to," she said.

"Except you were going to ditch."

"You don't know that for sure. You arrived early."

"Don't bullshit a bullshitter. You had no intention of coming down to find me."

"If you knew that, then why did you go through the trouble of this?" She swept a hand at the table.

"Because I know that you know that I'm here working, just like I know that you are here on a job."

"Says who?" Tanya exclaimed hotly.

"Says your mother."

That clamped her lips tight. "When were you talking to Mother?" And why had her handler opened her mouth?

"I didn't. Sherry, boss's wife, did."

"I'm not technically here on official business."

"Something about testing in the field was what I heard." He popped a chicken ball into his mouth, some of the cherry sauce catching his lip. She almost reached over to give it a lick.

"I'm refining a program that will clone signals and use them to piggy-back onto people's devices to filch any information and images stored."

"Shit. That's pretty cool. Does it work?" Devon asked.

She shrugged, acting casual but pleased by the praise. "That's what I'm hoping to find out. What about you?"

"Supposed to be locating some important player. We got a tip that he'd be here this weekend."

"You got a name? Maybe I can help," she offered without even thinking.

"I wish." He shook his head. "All I was given was a

location and a date. Apparently, the person I'm after is really private, as in no real name, no pictures."

"What's this guy done, do you know?"

"Nothing they've been able to prove, but apparently, he's connected to the buy and sell trade."

"What's wrong with that?"

"He's buying and selling other people's cars. My target has supposedly set up chop shops all over Quebec and Ontario, and he's been bribing law enforcement to stay out of his business."

"Wouldn't it just be easier to shut down his operation?"

"Yes, and no."

He didn't need to say more because she understood. Sometimes, even if you cut off the head of a crime syndicate, someone else just took their place.

"Seems like a lot of effort for illegal car trading."

"It is, except they've been going after more expensive vehicles, and a few of the owners—pretty, young ladies—have gone missing of late."

"Human trafficking?" she said with a twist of her lips.

"That's what the assumption is since none of their bodies have turned up. Given we want the head of the snake, and the location of the women if they're still alive, I'm here to see if I can spot him and bring him to justice."

Eyeing Devon, Tanya drummed her fingers on the table. "Could it be that guy we saw in the stairwell?"

Why else plant a jammer unless he wanted to hide something?

"I don't know, he gave off more of a minion vibe. I need to find out more, which is why I'm glad you're here. I'd like us to team up."

She couldn't help but groan. "Oh, no. I am not working with you again."

"Come on, Bunny. We kicked ass last time."

They had. But when Devon dove out that third-floor window of the bank, she'd not known if he survived. Had no idea about the wide ledge that he'd landed on. Had suffered through a heart-stopping moment when she thought he died, never mind finding out after the fact that he'd faked it. She'd not seen him since, and for good reason. He made her heart pound. And not just from adrenaline.

"I don't do takedowns." She kept to the safer side of jobs and stuck to hacking.

"You wouldn't actually have to do anything but help me figure out which of the guests I'm looking for."

"I'm sure you can figure that out on your own."

"I'll bet you can do it faster, though."

"So, you admit I have more expertise." She smirked.

"Are you fishing for compliments, Bunny?" He smiled. "Would it help if I said you're amazing?"

The statement flushed her with heat, but she still shook her head. "I can't get involved. For one thing, how would I explain to Skee why you keep hanging around."

"Who's Skee? Your boyfriend?"

For a second, she blinked at his assumption and then laughed. "It's my nickname for Cory. Skee, as in the great Gretzky."

"Oh. I'm easy to explain. Just tell your boy we're seeing each other."

"No." The answer shot out so quickly, it was a wonder he didn't go flying.

"It's the perfect solution. Then, we can meet up to exchange info without making anyone suspicious."

"Or, we could avoid each other and use this modern thing called texting."

"But that takes out all the fun of working together." He offered a smile that was at best boyish, at worst, panty-wetting.

"You seem to forget I'm not here for work, and even if I were, being close to you isn't my idea of fun," she hotly retorted. Conversing with Devon had an energizing effect, which led to confusion, especially since she didn't feel any guilt and rather yearned to say "*yes*" to his proposal.

"Why do you dislike me so much, Bunny?" Devon leaned in close.

Too close. She couldn't help but stare at his mouth. Remembering how it felt against hers.

"I don't dislike you." Her problem was her attraction to him.

"Really?" He reached out a hand, and she almost fell out of her chair avoiding his touch. "I rest my case," he said with a smirk.

She stood and tried to still the rapid beating of her heart. "I told you, I'm not into dating anyone."

"Because you're pining for a man dead fifteen years?" He rose from his seat and towered over her. "Are you that afraid of getting involved with someone?"

"You have no idea what you're talking about."

"Actually, I do. When I found out that my fiancée was cheating, it took me forever to date again."

Ouch. That wasn't a nice thing to do. "I'm sorry that happened to you, but my situation is not the same, not even close."

"We both lost people we loved. Difference is, I'm still looking for a second chance, while you're holding on to the past."

"You don't understand how hard it was for me when Antoine died." He couldn't grasp just how badly her life had taken a turn for the worse. Then again, in a sense, it had led to her life becoming amazing.

"Don't you think you've mourned long enough?"

The funny part was, she'd stopped thinking about Antoine a while ago. She could have dated if it didn't seem so complicated. It just became easier to use her dead boyfriend as an excuse. "Why does it matter if I have or not? You and I won't see each other once this weekend is done."

"True. So, why not let loose a bit, Bunny? Remember what it's like to live."

"By what? Having sex with you?"

His lips curved. "How about just having fun and seeing what happens?"

"I know what would happen. Not interested. And stop calling me Bunny. My name is Tanya!" She sought to dispel the intimacy the use of the nickname wrought.

"Don't you miss the touch of another person?" Devon asked, his gaze intent. "Haven't you craved the intimacy?"

Yes! And never more than now, not that she said anything. Deny. Deny. Deny. That was how she handled it. "How did we go from discussing your mission to my lack of a sex life?"

"Because I could taste your hunger in the kiss we shared."

"Could not!" she exclaimed. Could he?

"Please, Bunny. I thought you were going to melt into a puddle."

She snorted. "Now, you're imagining things." Hopefully, he didn't sense the lie.

"Are you saying you didn't feel anything?"

"Not a bit."

"Then you won't have a problem kissing me again."

Her gaze shot to his mouth even as she said, "I am not kissing you."

"Why not? You just said you didn't feel anything."

She could tell by his expression that he thought he had her. But she couldn't let him win. She had to prove to him—and herself—that the first kiss had just taken her by surprise. If she went into it eyes wide-open, she could control what happened.

"You're bossy. This is sexual harassment."

"I'm not touching you." He held up his hands. "I'm talking and asking real questions, to which you're lying."

Again, how did he know? "I'm not lying, and I can prove it." She leaned over, grabbed him by the cheeks, and yanked him close enough that she could plaster her mouth to his for a kiss. A quick slant, and then she let him go.

He snorted. "That's not a kiss. *This* is a kiss." He dragged her into his arms and took her mouth. Literally possessed it, nibbling and sucking and igniting a flame in her, stronger than anything she recalled.

Stole her breath. Her wits. Even any protest.

When he pulled away, she made a sound, and it took forever to raise her heavy lids.

"I should take a picture of your face just to make a point, but I won't. I expect your wet panties are evidence enough." He settled her back in her seat and stood, moving to the door where he shrugged on his coat.

"Where," she said in a voice too husky, "are you going?"

"For a cold shower. Because unlike you, I'm not afraid to admit you turn me on."

With that final statement, he left. And he was right.

There was no denying it.

Her panties were beyond wet, and the cold shower did nothing to fix her problem.

CHAPTER SEVEN

DEVON DIDN'T WANT to leave Tanya. Arousal heated him, and despite her protests, he could tell that she felt it, too. But if she were going to be stubborn about it, then he wasn't about to force her.

Not to mention, he was here to do a job, not seduce a woman who literally stole his breath—and wits.

The evening crowd had drifted off in the main lobby. It was the perfect time to find out the name of the guy they'd encountered in the stairwell. Someone Devon had a feeling might be his target. And, yes, he was stereotyping, because for all the bleeding hearts wanted to deny it, assholes tended to be easy to spot. Even if this guy weren't the one Devon was looking for, he could almost guarantee that the fellow was a bad shit.

Striding up to the front desk, the first thing Devon did was flash his fake private investigator license to the young lady with mascara so thick her eyelids must get a workout while batting them.

"Hey there, darling." He smiled. "I'm Devon Spade. PI on a case. I don't suppose you've got a guy staying here, about six foot-ish, bald with a goatee, kind of mean-looking? Would have arrived this afternoon."

"Oh, I really couldn't say." Said coyly with a rigorous bat of her lashes.

"Of course, you can't. Don't blame you one bit."

"If you gave me a name, I could ring his room for you," she offered.

"Except I highly doubt he's using his real name given he's up to no good. Are you sure you can't help me?" He slid a fifty-dollar bill across the counter.

Her eyes widened, and she snatched the cash. "Sounds like you're talking about Marcel Lavoie. Why are you looking for him?"

Devon laid it on thickly. "I was hired to find out if Mr. Lavoie is cheating on his wife and get pictures of his mistress if possible."

In response, the eyes behind the desk widened as the young woman gasped. "He doesn't have a mistress. He's staying with a man."

"You don't say. Tell me about him," Devon prodded, leaning on the desk. Turned out Melanie—as her nametag indicated—didn't know much. She only knew of the other guest because Marcel had asked for two keycards and mentioned that he'd be sharing with a friend.

"Then how do you know it's a man?" he asked.

"Because I saw him getting on the elevator with a dude."

Melanie also mentioned no housekeeping was to be conducted for the length of Marcel's stay. He was very specific about not wanting anyone in the room.

"I'm surprised they chose the third floor instead of one of the cabins if he wants privacy so bad," Devon remarked. The third floor had nothing special going for it. Not like the lavish sixth-floor penthouse suites. Coincidentally, Tanya's room was 205, which meant if the floor plan repeated itself on each level, her room sat directly below Marcel's. A one-bedroom suite with a single bed and a pullout.

Perhaps Marcel and his friend were gay lovers. Or good friends. In reality, other than their brief encounter in the stairwell, Devon knew nothing about the guy. Not a single shred. Could be Marcel and his companion weren't even Devon's targets. He had no real way of knowing until he dug deeper.

More than ever, he wished he were staying in the lodge rather than in a cabin that required a brisk five-minute walk in the cold.

Bunny has a room. That she shared with her kid. Technically, they could make it work. Tell the boy they were romantically involved. Yet Tanya had already said that was a no-go.

The kiss said she might change her mind, however.

A part of Devon wanted to go back up to her room and kiss her some more.

The idea bordered on madness but was tempting. So very damned tempting.

Which made it a bad idea. Given Devon's track record with women, should he even be thinking of getting involved with her?

She obviously wasn't one to take sex casually. There existed a time when he didn't either. Then Arabella had cheated on him. In his bed.

It had messed him up, and he'd had a few wild years. Even when those ended, people kept his reputation alive with supposition. Let them. The truth was, he'd not been involved with a woman since... Hmmm. A damned long time, once he thought about it.

Yet, here he was, flirting with a single mom who wanted to remain single, looking for an excuse to get close to her so she could shoot him down.

Sigh.

Maybe rather than mooning over Bunny, he should try doing his damned job. Since the signal on his phone remained active, he had to assume that Marcell—or someone else—hadn't planted another jamming device. Just in case, his crypto app was running in the background, making sure Tanya and her computer—or anyone else for that matter—couldn't hack his files.

No one needed to see the picture of him and his cat on Christmas. Pretty sad when the only thing under his decorated palm tree was a present for Pima. Short for Pain In My Ass. Sherry was currently babysitting his Siamese best friend.

Moving away from the front desk, Devon debated how to check on his possible suspect. He'd already texted the name to Bad Boy Inc.—BBI for short—to run through their computers, but if Marcel had used an alias, then he'd get nothing.

He needed something. Proof that this was the duo Devon was looking for.

Scrolling through his mobile apps with inane names like Door Quest—able to unlock any electronic door—and Road King—which could clone a fob-less car key in seconds—he came across the perfect one.

Big Ears. A sound-enhancing app. It was the perfect time of night for Devon to casually saunter down the third-floor hall to the ice machine at the far end. With his phone in hand, it could record and identify the faintest sounds. Could even interpret voices.

The app also did some other stuff like translate and do reverse voice something-or-other searches. Whatever the fuck that meant. When Mason started describing the features of his special apps, Devon's eyes glazed over. He liked to employ the KISS method when it came to equipment for missions. Keep it simple stupid. And that went for a hot bunny, too.

Getting involved was bad. Using her for info only was good.

Then again, given that some bad dudes might be staying here, he owed it to her to keep her in the loop on any developments in his mission—as a common courtesy to a fellow secret operative.

Pathetic how he managed to find reasons to go groveling back to see her already. Before he did, though, he should actually have something to report.

The main floor of the lodge had mostly cleared out. Even the boys were heading off to bed. They waited for the elevator, Cory among the bunch.

Devon looked at the large group and decided it best to use the stairs. Just before entering, he glanced at Cory. The boy missed the first cab due to it being too full, and the second elevator had yet to arrive. Of more interest—and a bit of concern—was that Marcel stood waiting, as well. Not a big deal. Cory wasn't exactly alone, given he still had some of his friends with him. A glance at the other faces didn't show anyone seemingly with the big guy.

Devon hurried up the stairs, feet pounding, taking them two at a time and making it up the flights with heart-pounding speed. He spilled onto the third floor, and marched quickly down the hall, heading for the elevator. He arrived just as it dinged. He dropped to tie his shoe and intentionally didn't make eye contact as the doors hummed open. An operative shouldn't be noticed when doing surveillance. Especially given that Marcel had already seen him that afternoon.

Just as he finished tying the bow, someone walked by. Slimmer-looking than expected in their light blue jeans. A quick glance showed a lanky kid sauntering up the hall, his upper body in a hunch. Definitely not Marcel, which meant the man remained on the elevator.

Why would he do that?

Back to the stairwell, Devon went, racing up one more flight, making it to the bend in the hall where he could see the elevator. It opened, and one kid stepped out. No Marcel.

Which could only mean...

He'd gotten off at the first stop on the second floor.

Fuck. Fuck. Fuck. Devon raced down the stairs, jumping the last three steps on each landing. Emerging on the second floor, he immediately glanced at door 205 in time to see it shut.

He quickly walked past it, his phone app active, and his own ears peeled, listening for signs of trouble. He almost bumped into Marcel as he turned the corner, heading to the elevator.

Devon didn't quite manage to duck his face in time.

"You again." Marcel scowled.

"Don't give me attitude." Devon had to think fast and chose to go on the attack. "You're the one who cock-blocked me this afternoon."

Marcel sneered. "I was doing the woman a favor. A hot number like her deserves better than a make out session in a dirty stairwell."

"Don't judge me for smooching with my girl where I can. She hasn't told her kid about me yet," Devon confided in a hushed tone of voice. "Makes it hard to, you know..." Devon arched a brow.

"I do know now." Marcel grimaced.

Having established a weak comradery, Devon prodded. "What are you really doing on this floor? You trying to bang one of the hockey moms, too?"

"No." Marcel stepped past him and headed up the hall in the direction of Tanya's room.

Devon followed. "Sorry. That was sexist. You might be into dads."

"I am not dating a man," Marcel seethed.

"Chill, dude. No one cares in this day and age."

"Out of my way."

Marcel shoved at Devon, but he didn't budge. He wasn't a pushover. "You never did say why you're on this floor."

"I didn't say, because I don't have to."

"Actually, you kind of do. Lots of families with kids on this floor. Yet I haven't seen you with a child. Matter of fact, last time I saw you was on the third floor, not the second."

"I could say the same."

"I was in the stairwell making out with my woman. What are you doing?"

"Since you're a nosy fucker, I was getting ice. Our machine isn't working." The most convenient cover in the world.

"You forgot to bring the ice bucket to get some."

"My bad."

"Guess you better go grab it."

"What I do is none of your business, asshole," Marcel snapped.

"I'm making it my business."

"You are irritating me," Marcel grumbled. "And I don't take well to being annoyed."

"Too fucking bad." Devon intentionally needled him. The best way to take a measure of someone was to push every single last button they owned.

In this case, Marcel snapped, and a gun emerged. "I've had enough of you."

Devon eyeballed the weapon aimed at him. "You know, Canada, including Quebec, doesn't allow for concealed carry, right?"

A smirk crossed Marcel's face. "Do I look like a motherfucker who cares?"

"The problem nowadays is that no one cares about the laws." Devon shook his head. "Which is why it is up to individuals like me to uphold them." He wrapped his fingers around Marcel's wrist, which only served to bring the gun closer.

"I will shoot," Marcel hissed.

"Go ahead. It would be pretty dumb given we're in a public place, asshole. And who's to say someone isn't watching?"

"There are no cameras."

"No, but there are people, and you should know, these hotel hallways are like funnels when it comes to sound.

"You were mugging me. It was self-defense." Marcel still smiled.

"Did you just try and call me a thief?" Devon dug his fingers in and applied pressure, hard enough that Marcel's eyes widened in pain.

"Motherfucker, let go." Marcel might have tried to fire, only he couldn't as Devon pressed a nerve in his thumb, then the back of his hand, which caused Marcel's grip to loosen.

Devon snatched the gun from him and dumped the clip.

"Hand it back." Marcel lunged, but Devon danced out of reach.

"Don't be a sore loser. I won fair and square. Just saved you from going to jail, too. You're welcome."

"I'll pulp you with my bare hands," Marcel growled.

"Why the anger, dude?" Devon asked. "I was just making sure you were gonna leave, and now that I know you're packing, I'm glad I stuck around. Hate for you to shoot the wrong person."

"You'll pay for this."

A door swung open, and an irritated female voice said, "Do you guys mind keeping it down? My kid is trying to sleep." Tanya stepped out, looking young and adorably comfortable in her t-shirt and track pants. Her son stepped out behind her.

Devon had to quickly tuck the gun behind his

back. But he couldn't hide Marcel, nor shut the guy's big fat mouth.

"This must be the ignorant child. The one who doesn't know. Not for long." Marcel snorted. "Guess what, kid. Your mother is whoring it up behind your back with him." Marcel jabbed a finger at Devon. "Might be time you started calling him Daddy."

"Mom?" There was a questioning note in the single syllable.

Devon could see that Tanya wanted to kill him. The tight set of her shoulders said it, and he half expected her to throw him under Marcel—and his rather bus-like bulk—rather than reply.

But she surprised him. "Yes, Skee. It's true. Devon is my boyfriend. We were planning to tell you on this trip."

The fact that she managed to actually confirm his impromptu lie made him want to kiss her. He moved in her direction, away from Marcel. "So glad that's out in the open," he declared, smiling at Cory, who frowned.

"You're dating my mom? Why keep it a secret?"

Tanya jumped in. "I wasn't sure how to tell you."

"How about, hey Corey, I found this cool dude and we're hooking up." Corey rolled his eyes. "Geez, mom. Even I have a girlfriend. It's not a big deal."

Devon slid an arm around Tanya. "Does this mean I get to spend the night?"

"No!" she hotly exclaimed, whereas the kid...

"You wanna sleep over? Sure." Cory shrugged. "But I'm not sharing the couch."

Devon couldn't decide what was funnier, the nonchalant way the kid tossed that out there, or Tanya's face.

Marcel laughed for him. "Hope you remember how thin the walls and doors are tonight when you try defiling her around her son."

Tanya's cheeks turned red. Devon's might have a bit, too.

"Time you left," he said. "Boy's gotta sleep before the big game tomorrow."

They all watched as Marcel scowled his way around the corner. Only then did Devon sigh. "Sorry about that. I caught him skulking and wanted to know what was up."

"Dude is creepy," Cory stated. "Good thing you're here to watch over my mom."

"I would have been fine," Tanya retorted.

Cory gave Devon a look, the kind that drove women insane because it assumed they needed protection. Devon did his best not to choke on his laughter as the boy headed into the room.

But Tanya caught it. "Not one word."

"Wouldn't dream of it," Devon muttered, following her inside.

Entering the room he'd left not that long ago, he noticed the boy flopped on the couch, phone in hand, not paying them any mind. But he had no doubt that the kid was listening, which meant a careful choice of words.

"Sorry the news about our relationship came out like that, Bunny."

"Ha, I should have known," Cory said with a snort. "I mean, my mom never hits anyone, and the first thing she did was toss you in a snowbank."

"Only because she caught me off guard." A vain attempt to defend his manhood.

"He deserved it," Tanya hastily added. "I told him I wasn't ready to tell you yet. It's too soon."

"I'm not a baby, Mom." Cory shot her a glare. "You don't have to hide it."

Devon almost winced. "She just wanted to protect you."

"From what? People date all the time."

"You know I didn't want to disrespect your father," she said, hands tucked behind her back, probably to stop herself from throttling Devon.

Cory snorted. "Mom, it's morbid how long you've been single."

"You know, now that it's out in the open, you and Cory probably have to talk." Devon began to inch away from a situation he'd caused and now regretted. "I'll head back to my cabin. Do some work." Perhaps the recording he'd gotten of Marcel's voice would ring a bell in a database somewhere. Not to mention, he was pretty sure Tanya wanted to kill him. Best to get far, far away.

"Why would you leave now that I know?" Cory lifted his head from his phone and stared at them.

"It wouldn't be appropriate for him to stay," Tanya said primly.

"But, Mom, it's snowing outside. And cold, too. I mean, you are dating, right?" Cory asked. "Now you won't have to feed me lame decorating excuses to hang out."

"You caught me," was her flat reply. "I was looking for the right way to break it to you. Now that it's happened, Devon is right, we should talk about it. Alone."

"Talk about what, Mom?" Cory glanced at her. "I think it's cool you're finally dating again. He seems like an okay kind of guy. Just don't turn into Tommy's mom."

Devon might not understand the reference but got the gist from her red cheeks.

"Cory!"

"What?" The kid grinned. "You're the one who called her that name. Not me."

It didn't take much to guess the name. Since Devon had caused this mother-son tiff, it was time for him to diffuse it and take his punishment like a man. Surely, she wouldn't kill him with her kid nearby.

Devon clapped his hands. "Glad you're being so cool with this. Why don't I take your mom into the other room and let her talk at me instead of you? I'm a big man, I can handle it." Devon rolled his eyes and sighed as if suffering.

Tanya's gaze narrowed.

Cory went back to his phone with a casual, "Whatever. Try not to be too loud. I gotta get some sleep for my game tomorrow."

Lips pursed, Tanya silently stomped to the bedroom and grabbed the television remote, turning it on to some drama in progress. She waited until the door was closed then grabbed hold of his shirt to haul him close and whisper, "I don't fucking believe you. I told you I didn't want to be your pretend girlfriend."

The crass language sounded all too sexy coming from her lips. "I didn't do it on purpose."

"Really? Then what the heck were you doing in that hall with the guy from the stairs?"

"I was following him."

"He's staying on this floor?"

"Nope. Third level, according to the front desk, and yet I found him skulking around this floor. Claims he was getting ice, but I doubt that. Would you feel better if I told you I have confirmation that he's not a nice guy?" He removed the gun he'd tucked into his waistband under his shirt. "He pulled this on me."

She grabbed it and turned it over in her hands. "This is a serious weapon."

"No kidding." Devon grabbed it and popped out the clip. "Armor-piercing bullets. Not something you can buy in Canada."

"Illegal ammo. And he pulled it awful quick," she noted.

"How would you know?"

A smirk tilted her lips as she pointed to the laptop sitting on the bed. "Part of my security involves a camera and mic by all the entrances to the room and a few more eyes in the hall."

"So, you saw everything?"

"And heard. Cock-blocking? Really?" She eyed him sternly.

"I'm a guy. I had to make it sound believable. And I think Marcel bought it."

"The weird part is, Cory also believes we've been secretly dating. And he's fine with it." She glanced at the door with a frown. "I would have expected more pushback from him."

"Maybe he's tired of seeing you alone."

"Or he knows we're faking and wants to see how far we'll go."

At that, Devon laughed. "Come on, seriously? He's just a kid."

"A smart kid," she muttered. She focused her gaze on Devon. "You used the name, Marcel."

"That is our stairwell friend's name."

"Did you happen to get a last name?" she asked.

"Lavoie."

She sprawled across the bed and began typing on her laptop. Devon fought an urge to join her.

"According to the hotel registry, he is in room—"

"Three oh five," Devon interrupted. "With a friend. No name."

"He's booked at the lodge until Monday morning. Let's see what else we can find out about Marcel."

"Not much," he advised. "Mason at BBI was trying to dig up some dirt but couldn't find anything with a quick search. On the surface, the guy is clean as a whistle."

"Too clean," Tanya remarked. "Which makes him suspicious. Especially since he's already got one illegal gun. What else is Marcel hiding?"

"I'd still like to know why he was on this floor," Devon mused aloud. "The ice was a bullshit excuse since he went straight from the lobby to the second level."

"You think he was up to no good," she stated.

"He did have a gun."

"Question is, does he have another, and what was his intent? Did you find out anything about the person staying with him?"

Devon shook his head. "Didn't have a chance. And I probably shouldn't wander around anymore tonight, or he will get suspicious. I'll see what I can find once I'm back in my room."

"Leaving so soon?"

"We both know you don't want me to stay."

"Cory's expecting you to stick around, though. If you don't, it will look suspicious."

"Then I'll stay." Even if the invitation came begrudgingly.

"What are we going to do?" She glanced at the bed and bit her lower lip adorably.

Another kind of guy might have suggested something dirty, but knowing her history... "Don't worry about sharing. I can sleep on either side."

She cast him a quick glance, then eyed the floor, her cheeks hot with color.

It entranced the hell out of him, which might be why he kept teasing. "I hope you don't snore. Oh, and I usually sleep naked."

"Not tonight, you're not!" she huffed. "If you wait until Cory is asleep, you can sneak out."

"How long will that be?"

She shrugged.

"Then I'm getting comfortable." He stretched out on her bed, being careful beside her laptop. He closed his eyes and said nothing.

Tanya sighed. "Why me?" The bed jiggled a bit as she moved the laptop off it and then, to his surprise, lay down beside him.

The television went to a commercial, and she said softly, "Do you know, when we shared that hotel room in Vancouver, it was the first time I'd ever slept with a man."

"We each had our own bed."

"In the same room, though," she corrected.

"Hold on." He rolled to his side and looked at her.

"You mean you've never actually spent the night with a guy? Not even Cory's dad?"

She shook her head. "We were teenagers when we dated. Both still living at home. We never spent the night together anywhere."

"Shiiiiit," Devon muttered, only to realize how it might sound. "Not to say you're weird or anything. Okay, you are, but only in the sense that you really haven't experienced anything."

"I don't know if I'd say that. I've been through a lot."

"I'm sure you have, having a kid, and then getting head-hunted for KM and all. I'm talking relationships."

"Let me guess, you have tons of experience."

"Some. You don't get to thirty-eight and not have some idea."

"Have you slept with a lot of women?" She eyed him, and he wanted to squirm.

"Yeah," he muttered. "But I should add, I've only actually cared for a few, and loved only one."

"You prefer casual sex."

"No," he hastened to correct. "It's more...I think I expect too much. I told you, I loved one woman."

"The one who cheated?"

"Yeah, and to this day, I don't get why she betrayed me. I thought we had our shit together as a couple. We were making plans. Having sex. Sharing everything." Including a few of his casual friends, apparently. A good friend would have turned her down and told him so he'd have the satisfaction of tossing her out. Instead, he'd returned early from a trip to find Arabella and Les in bed. His bed. He'd burned the sheets. Then the mattress.

"Antoine and I were like that. Best of friends. We met in the computer club at school. We were going to run off together, get a place, and leave our stamp on the world."

"How did he die?"

"Stupidly." She sighed. "He went snowmobiling, and despite being warned to stay off the ice, he went out onto the lake. They found one of his gloves by the edge of a hole in the ice. They dredged the lakebed and found the machine in the spring."

"Then you found out you were pregnant. And kept the baby," Devon said, filling in the next blank.

"Managed to finish high school before my parents noticed. That's when they kicked me out."

"You're kidding." His eyes widened. "What assholes." He almost winced as the words escaped, but Tanya smiled.

"Yeah, they are assholes. Because of them, I bounced around a lot. Especially once Cory was born."

"And you never once dated?" He still had a hard time getting over that point.

"Never wanted to." Her lips turned in a sad tilt. "Thought there was something wrong with me for a while."

"I know the feeling. I just didn't entertain it as long

as you did. After Arabella and I broke up, I tried moving on, but no one really caught my interest. There was something, I don't know, lacking in them." None of them had ignited a spark like he had with Arabella.

Now, he saw it for the tiny thing it was, considering the inferno that engulfed him whenever he was around Tanya.

"I felt guilty," Tanya admitted. "Poor Antoine was dead. It didn't seem right to just forget him and move on."

"Except that would have been normal."

Her lips pursed. "Maybe, like you, the problem was I never saw anyone that I thought could take his place."

"Do you even know what you're looking for?"

"I'm not looking."

He reached out to tuck a strand of hair behind her ear. "Everyone is looking. You only stop when you find the person that completes you."

"Do you think you'll ever find them?"

Looking into her eyes, he could honestly say, "Yes."

Perhaps she read something in his gaze because she flipped over. "Try not to wake us when you leave."

He smiled at her back. She might not want to admit it, but he suspected that she felt the same kind of burning need he did when they were together.

It made him wonder what would happen if he were to reach out to her right now and drape his arm over her waist. Maybe snuggle in close, spooning her into his body. How he wanted to nuzzle her hair and breathe hotly against her ear. Let his hands roam over the shape of her.

Fuck.

All these thoughts only served to make him hard. So fucking hard.

But he didn't act.

Tanya had opened up to him. Spilled her innermost feelings. Heavy shit. And for all his flirting, he didn't know if he could, in good conscience, seduce her.

Tanya wasn't just any woman. She was a mother. A fighter.

And he was...probably not the right kind of guy for her. But he wanted to be.

At two a.m., he rose from the bed, wanting to stay but knowing he had to leave. He tiptoed out, past the boy snoring on the couch.

Once he reached the outdoors, the cold air proved a brisk slap to his lungs, but he inhaled it deeply, trying to clear his mind and senses of Tanya. It and the still-falling snow were probably why he never heard the person coming up behind him to clock him on the head.

CHAPTER EIGHT

DEVON WAS GONE by the time Tanya woke the next day. Probably a good thing given her cheeks were a bright red as she realized that she'd slept with a man!

Fully clothed, each on their own side of the bed, but they'd shared a mattress, and she'd fallen asleep thinking of him. At one point, she'd woken, body wrapped caterpillar style in the blanket, spooned into him, his heavy arm draped over her. It'd felt nice.

Damned nice.

Which was why it was best that he'd disappeared before she woke. She might have forgotten that Cory slept in the other room and done what every movie in creation made look sexy...morning nookie. Even though the idea of sex of any kind daunted. It had been so long. Would she remember how? What if she sucked at it?

She had only one man to draw her experience

from. Let's say she could let go enough to have sex with Devon, it would probably be only once because a man with his experience would be appalled at how badly she performed.

"Ugggh." She buried her face in the pillow as she groaned her frustration, then froze as a husky male voice said, "Your boy says you take your coffee with a hint of chocolate in it."

Turning her head, she squinted at Devon. "You're still here."

"Where else would I be?" Then he tossed over his shoulder, "Is your mom always this slow in the morning?"

"She's more of a night owl. She's always up working," Skee, the traitor, announced before popping his head in and tossing her a wide grin. "Wake up, Mummy." The word he used when he teased. "We've got to be at the arena in forty-five minutes."

"I need coffee and food." The first was thrust at her in a styrofoam cup. The second emerged from the paper bag Devon held in the other hand.

"Is that—?"

"A maple crème donut? Damned straight, it is." He smiled as he took a bite, then outright laughed when she lunged for it. She polished it off in record time, quickly enough that he only managed three bites of his other donut before she stole that one, too.

Only then did she lean back in bed and groan as she sipped her coffee. The door remained open as

Devon sat on the edge of her bed. "I don't know if I'm aroused or disturbed," he murmured.

"Devon!" she exclaimed, glancing at the doorway.

"Don't worry. He's in the bathroom getting ready."

"Why are you back so quick?"

He said softly, "My room had a problem last night."

"Oh?"

"Management says it looks like the pellet stove door wasn't properly shut, and a spark from it ignited the cabin." He paused. "With me in it."

"What?" She scrambled to her knees. "What really happened?"

"Someone bonked me on the head when I was walking back and then tossed me inside before setting the fire."

"How did you get out?"

"Hard noggin." He tapped it. "I woke, smelled the smoke, and crawled out. They found me in a snowbank."

"And your room?"

"Toast. As are my things. The hotel was kind enough to give me a place to shower and some clean clothes."

"Who did this?"

"Who do you think?" was his sardonic reply.

"Did they toss your room before setting it on fire? Did you have anything that might give you away?" Anything that would lead trouble to her and Cory?

"Nothing but clothes and toiletries. I keep my

weapons on me, usually, and everything else is on my phone. Which is missing."

"Oh, dear."

"Not really. I have a spare, and the one they stole is thumbprint activated. Soon as anyone fucks with it, it's programmed to wipe itself, or so Mason claims."

"Could just be a random act of violence. Robbery, even."

"Yup."

But given her and Devon's occupation, it seemed unlikely. "Did the hotel give you another room?"

"They can't. They're full."

Before she could slap herself out of it, she said, "Since we've already established you as my boyfriend, you should stay with me." Only belatedly did she add, "And Cory."

"Why, Bunny, I'd be delighted."

"But don't mess with my kid," Tanya warned.

"Whatever do you mean?"

"No made-up sex stories."

"I take it real ones are okay?"

"No. He's fourteen, and you shouldn't be talking dirty with him."

"Can I talk dirty with you?" Spoken with a devilish grin.

"No," she sputtered. "I need you to not be you while you stay with me."

"Which means what exactly?"

"No daredevil stuff."

"I'm a changed man, Bunny. Anything else?"

"Just because we're pretending to be boyfriend and girlfriend doesn't mean you do stuff with him."

"Stuff, as in?"

"Fatherly things. I don't want you messing him up since you won't be around for long."

"And what if I were? Would we be allowed to have a snowball fight and play Black Ops together?" he mocked.

Her lips pressed into a line. "You're making fun of me."

"Yup. Because you're being crazy."

"I can't help it. I'm worried about Cory."

"The boy will be fine. It's his mother I'm worried about." Devon leaned over to pluck her empty cup from her hand. Their gazes caught, which was when Cory walked in.

"Whoa, didn't mean to interrupt. Put a sock on the door, would you."

"Skee!" Tanya's cheeks exploded with heat.

"I'm going over to the arena now to get ready. Freddy's mom is giving me a ride, so take your time." Her boy winked before leaving.

Devon snorted. "And you're worried about me corrupting him?"

"Teenagers are much more knowledgeable than we used to be at their age," she mumbled.

"Feeling old, Bunny?"

Looking at Devon, his eyes dancing with humor,

she had to say that for the first time in a long time, she didn't feel old at all. As a matter of fact, she'd not felt this giddy since...she was dating Antoine.

Once the door to the room closed, she shoved at Devon. "I need to check on how my signal collector did overnight."

"You know, a less confident man would feel reject-ed." Devon sprawled on the bed as she tugged her computer onto her lap.

"Considering I just asked you to be my fake boyfriend and share a room with me, you should be feeling on top of the world."

"Actually, I am feeling pretty good." He winked. "What time's Cory's first game?"

"Eight."

He glanced at his watch. "I'll meet you there. I'm going to see what I can salvage from my room and buy from the shop. If you see Marcel, watch but don't be obvious."

"I'm not new at this," she sassed. "By the time I see you, I might even know what he's hiding. The scan finished overnight, which means I've got lots of data to work with."

"Do you really think your geeky tricks will net faster results than my slow and steady observation? After all, who discovered Marcel's name first?"

"I did." She winked. "The moment we ran into him in the stairwell. But it's cute when you think you're smarter than me." She patted his cheek in a moment of boldness that almost flustered. But she pulled it off and left him sitting there slack-jawed.

She didn't lock the door while she showered. Not because she expected Devon to join. Brash as he might be, he had honor.

Pity, because a part of her might not have minded.

Alas, the door remained shut. Tanya emerged, fully dressed, to find the suite empty. But he'd left her a note.

Bunny,

I'll bring you hot cocoa when I meet you at the game.

Smooches, your bear.

Bear? Had he seriously tried to give himself a studly nickname? "That's not how it works." She'd have to come up with something suitably annoying for him.

But the note was damned cute. It made Tanya wonder if it was entirely an act, or if Devon truly wrote dorky notes like that for his real girlfriends.

She didn't have much time before she needed to get to the arena. Work was all well and good, but her kid always came first.

KM was understanding in that respect. They didn't just give single mothers a hand up, they expected them to speak up. Some might misunderstand and think KM took advantage of vulnerable women. But the truth was, they taught the lost like

Tanya how to become independent, to rely on themselves, and to always put their kids first.

Was it any wonder she loved working for them?

The Big Sister program had rolled into another subroutine, this time matching signals to guests, paying extra special attention to those that she couldn't pair. She was hoping to pin down Marcel's phone and whatever electronics he and his friend might have brought. Then the hacking fun would begin.

But first. Hockey.

She drove to the arena, wondering if Devon knew how to get here. His problem, not hers. She cursed as she wandered around looking for a parking spot. Even this early, the recreation center was in full swing as everyone arrived to register for the tournament.

The boys were already on the ice warming up. The first game of the day meant skating on a crisp surface that'd had all night to harden. *Swish. Clack.*

The blades cut into the ice as they trailed their sticks, then slapped at pucks, aiming at a goalie that was more interested in stretching than stopping flat, round bullets.

Since she had a few minutes, she stood in line and waited to buy godawful, put-hair-on-your-chest arena coffee. No amount of creamer and sugar could fix it, but it was a staple for tournaments.

Sipping at it, she debated going into the arena and sitting on a cold bench, or she could stand a bit longer in the lobby where it was warm and watch through the window.

Maybe she was getting old. Used to be, she sat in the cold arena from the moment she arrived until the moment Cory left the ice. She used to swell with such pride and excitement when he came out to play.

She still did, but now it was tempered by the realization of how big he was getting. Smelly, too. How her child could come off the ice reeking so badly, she kept the windows rolled down so they could breathe, was beyond her.

But she loved his smelly, scrawny ass.

"What number is he?" It startled her to realize that Devon had snuck up beside her. She'd assumed that he was another hockey parent going for the prime viewing space.

"Six."

"He's fast."

"And tricky." She smiled with pride. "He's been skating since he was three. Holding a stick even younger than that. I gave him his first one at Christmas when he was just over a year old. It was orange with a foam grip. He slept with it every night, tucked close."

"Born to play."

"He's got a gift for sports, which is funny because I am the clumsiest thing." Her nose wrinkled. "I was always better with puzzles and machines than putting one foot in front of the other."

"I have a hard time believing that."

"I'm not too bad anymore. Mother helped me learn to balance on my own two feet." She smiled.

"See, for me, I was good at the sports stuff, not as great with my head. I used to rush in."

"And now?"

He cast her a serious glance. "Now, I like to take my time, make sure I'm doing the right thing."

The words held two meanings, and she knew it. As Devon had clearly intended.

"Nice move, Skee!" Devon suddenly cheered, drawing her attention to the ice.

She wasn't surprised to see Cory moving well. He had an uncanny ability to know where to go before the opposing player even knew he was headed there. It made him an effective defenseman.

Intent on the game, Devon rooted for him and paid Tanya no mind at all. It was disconcerting and endearing all at once. And Cory noticed. When a whistle blew, he intentionally skated past the viewing window and waved, grinning around his bright pink mouthguard.

"Hot shit, he's playing well," Devon exclaimed. "We are kicking ass."

"I agree. That boy is amazing on skates. You must be proud."

The voice froze her. Especially because it seemed familiar and yet utterly strange all at once. She whirled to see a man. But not just any man.

The hair was trimmed tight to his head, the ratty t-shirt replaced by a full suit under a thick, wool trench. But those eyes. She'd recognize those eyes anywhere.

It couldn't be. He was dead. Yet she still foolishly muttered, "Antoine? Is that you?"

The ghost from her past had the nerve to say, "Hi, Tanya. It's been a while."

Was it any wonder she slapped him?

CHAPTER NINE

TANYA'S HAND hit the guy's cheek with a loud crack. What Devon didn't get was the why part, not until he really looked at the guy and saw in his features an older version of the kid on the ice.

Possibly a relative, but given the seething anger and shock in Tanya? Shit. Was he looking at a dead man?

Tanya confirmed it a second later. "I see the reports about your demise were false." She sounded cool, but Devon could see the tension in her frame, and hear the simmering anger barely kept under control.

"Yeah, sorry about that."

"Sorry? You let everyone think you were dead." A bitter laugh emerged from Tanya, verging on hysterical. Her fingers crept into her coat pocket.

Would she shoot the guy in front of witnesses? Devon needed to steady her before she did something she regretted. "Tanya?" Just her name, but enough of a reminder that she exhaled, and her fingers moved away from her pocket.

"Devon, I'd like you to meet my ex-boyfriend, Antoine. The one I—and everyone else in my hometown—thought was dead."

A man now resurrected, which meant he didn't know about Cory, and given Tanya's pinched expression, Devon got the impression she wasn't keen on telling.

His turn to itch for a gun. Killing Antoine now before the kid found out would be the simplest solution. Any man who would disappear and make everyone think he'd died didn't deserve a kid as cool as Cory.

Which meant keeping the news about the boy hush-hush for the moment. Only one problem. How to explain why they were at a kid's hockey game?

A plan quickly formed as Devon thrust himself between Tanya and Antoine, drawing the focus to him and giving Tanya time to compose herself. "Shit, you are literally the walking dead. What an asshole thing to do, making folks think you died."

Brown eyes that somehow managed to look icy perused Devon. "And you are?"

"Her boyfriend. Devon." He forced the guy to shake his hand, even though he wouldn't get any DNA trace given that Antoine wore leather gloves.

But he'd find a way. Not because he doubted paternity. Devon could see too many similarities in the face. However, he did wonder if Antoine's genetic code existed in a database somewhere. Because a guy shouldn't be able to disappear for fifteen years without a trace.

"Imagine running into you here," Antoine said.

"Imagine running into you at all. I didn't realize the zombie apocalypse had arrived." Tanya's dry reply showed she'd regained some of her composure.

The guy didn't even have the courtesy to look a little abashed that he'd suddenly popped up. "Surprise?"

"Don't you dare try and be cute about this. Why did you fake your death?" Tanya snapped.

"I had my reasons for leaving the way I did."

"Without a word to anyone?" Tanya crossed her arms and wore a sour expression.

"It was best that way."

"It was cruel, at least to me," she spat.

"And for that, I'm sorry. I've regretted it, but it was necessary." Antoine intonated all the right words, even managed to look serious, and yet, Devon couldn't help but notice the inauthenticity.

The guy didn't mean a word of the bullshit. However, did Tanya realize it?

Moving away from the window where other parents were beginning to eye them with interest, she headed for a quiet spot and hissed at Antoine, "Where have you been?"

"Here and there. You're looking good."

A compliment that, as her fake boyfriend, Devon should address. "Bunny always looks good, don't you, baby?" Devon snared her around the waist and drew her close.

To his surprise, she didn't stab him in the kidney with a knife. Rather, she leaned into him. "Now sugar cheeks, you know you're biased."

Sugar cheeks? He almost burst out laughing. "Only the truth, Bunny. Which is why I'm shocked this guy actually had the strength to leave you. I am never letting you go." He stared down at her, a strange sincerity in the words that brought puzzlement to her gaze—and a pink hue to her cheeks.

"Devon, we have an audience," she tittered before turning her gaze back on Antoine.

"Sorry, I just can't help myself." He really couldn't, which might explain his next poke. "I guess I should thank Antoine for ditching you. Otherwise, I might never have met my hunny bunny."

The hand she'd slid around his waist on the inside of his jacket dug fingers into his side, hard enough to make him wince, and yet he grinned at Antoine's sour expression.

"What are you doing here?" Antoine asked.

"I could ask the same of you," she countered.

Rather than reply, Antoine looked past her to the

viewing window and the players flashing past. "Someone at my hotel mentioned there was a local tournament, and I thought I'd come watch." An assessing gaze turned on Tanya. "Your kid playing?"

Feeling Tanya stiffen by his side, Devon spoke quickly. "My son, actually. From my first marriage. It didn't work out so good. She was a liar. Kind of like you." The jab poked Antoine again. Keeping the attention away from Bunny proved imperative.

"You're here for your son," spoken flatly with an expression that gave nothing away.

This was the guy Tanya had been pining for?

"Yup. Lucky me, he and Tanya get along great. She's practically a mother to him." Devon kept an intent expression as she dug her fingers in again. "Bunny is his biggest fan and comes to all his games. Hell, she's so involved, she even makes cookies for his class at school." Yeah, he laid it on thick.

Antoine's flat gaze perused him, but he said nothing.

Tanya jumped in. "Cory's a great kid. Because he's got the best dad." She layered it on even thicker and hugged Devon's arm.

Antoine's expression turned stony. "I'm sure he is." Then to Tanya only, with a smile meant to soften her stance, he said, "It was really nice to run into you. We should have dinner and catch up."

"If I do, will you tell me why you ran away like a coward?" she sassed.

A hint of a smile curved Antoine's lips. "You'd have to meet me to find out."

"I'm here with my boyfriend. It wouldn't be appropriate."

"Bring the boyfriend and his son. I'd love to meet the child that you've taken to mothering."

Was that a hint of mockery in his tone? Before Tanya could jump in, Devon spoke, "Not today, mate. We've got team commitment stuff to do. Maybe Sunday when the tournament is over."

"I'm afraid my business will be done by then. Given my time is short, I'm sure you won't mind if Tanya and I sneak off together to catch up on old times." A slick side-step.

"Actually, I do mind. She's my girlfriend, and I won't have some old flame trying to put the moves on her." Devon pulled the macho card.

Tanya hissed, "As if I'd let him."

"And Tanya is in agreement to this? Still letting others dictate to you? You always were good at taking orders."

Antoine finally struck back, and judging by the indrawn breath by his side, it almost snapped Tanya.

Before she went all John Wick on the fellow's ass— her favorite movie, according to a texted tip he'd received anonymously—Devon chose to step in. "Dude, you treated her like shit. She has no interest in seeing you. Not after what you did. Leave her alone."

"We've got to go," Tanya snapped.

"Yeah, we're in charge of getting the boys, er—" Devon paused.

She helped him. "Gatorade to replenish their fluids. Bye, Antoine."

Devon was pleased that she didn't turn around to check out her old boyfriend.

She waited until they were loaded down with drinks and headed for the locker room before hissing, "What the heck was all that macho crap forbidding me from meeting with Antoine?"

"Just making our cover story believable."

"So believable you wrecked my chance of getting answers as to why Antoine did what he did."

"You can thank me later because I don't think you were going to like those answers."

She cast him a side-eye. "Don't tell me you think I'd fall victim to him again?"

"Well, you did stay celibate for fifteen years in honor of his memory."

Lips twisted, she muttered, "Thanks for reminding me. I am going to hear about this from my friends."

"I don't suppose your friends are in the habit of texting tidbits about you."

"Excuse me?" She shifted her grip on the box with drinks. Being independent and strong, she'd insisted on carrying half of them.

"How do you feel about *John Wick*?"

Rather than answer, her lips pinched. "What else did you get as a tidbit?"

"Chinese food is your favorite. You like to sing along with opera. You hate snakes, but love cats. I have a cat."

"I don't."

"Because the one you had died, and you've been reluctant to replace Miss Mittens."

The scowl proved epic. "I am going to kill them."

"Who?"

"My sisters. Mother must have told them you were here."

"Do they make a habit of texting strangers and telling them to hit on you?"

"Apparently, they've decided to do something about my single state." Her lips turned down.

"You think they're trying to set you up?"

Laughter emerged. "Totally. But it won't work." Any elation he'd started to feel deflated.

"Because you're still in love with Antoine." This time, he poked her, and she reacted.

"No," she spat. "That man means nothing to me."

"Are you sure about that?" He glanced at the locker room door. They could hear the buzz of conversation and the occasional raucous chuckle.

"Antoine doesn't know. Thanks to you. How did you know to fake it?"

"Given we don't know the deal with your ex, I thought it best we keep Cory's parentage on the down low."

"It is strange running into him after all this time. I wonder why he was at the arena," Tanya mused aloud.

"If I were to wager a guess? He was there for a kid."

"What makes you say that?"

"Because even though he was wearing gloves, you could see the outline of his wedding ring."

CHAPTER TEN

THE NEWS that Antoine might have gotten married and had a kid couldn't compare to the shock that he was alive in the first place. Not even close. The moment Tanya had seen him, she'd gone through a myriad of emotions.

First was disbelief. *I can't believe he's alive.*

A moment of elation. *Cory has a father.*

Followed by terror. *Oh my God, what if he tries to take Cory from me?*

Then anger. *How dare he never let anyone know he lived? What kind of asshole fakes his death?*

He didn't even have the courtesy to look ashamed of his actions.

Tanya couldn't think of a single good reason why a person would do that. Especially someone who had declared himself so in love with her that he would die without her.

After the cops had declared Antoine dead, Tanya felt guilty that she hadn't expired and joined him. After all, he'd made the pledge.

"I'll love you forever and ever. Even when I'm dead," Antoine had promised the first time they had sex.

Which in retrospect, was probably a speech to get her pants off.

And did it really count? We were both just kids. She was seventeen, and him a worldly nineteen, a previous dropout who'd returned to finish grade twelve and graduate. A rebel in many ways, yet Antoine still lived with his parents. Not that she'd ever met them. He had a litany of reasons why, starting with the fact that they weren't his real parents.

The first time she'd seen them was in an article in a paper, a nice-looking yuppy couple who said all the right things from the front step of a suburban house, distraught at the loss of their boy. It had confused Tanya at the time because Antoine had given the impression that they were trash. But smiling for the cameras didn't mean they were nice behind closed doors. She only had to think of her own family to know how they could hide from the world.

Apparently, Antoine had learned the art of hiding very well, given that she'd never even had an inkling that he might still be alive. Not to mention, he'd intentionally left her in the dark all these years. If he'd wanted to escape so badly, why not just tell her and give her the option of leaving with him?

The truth proved stark and painful.

He never loved me. Not like Tanya had loved him.

Which meant she'd spent fifteen years being faithful to a lie.

And now had a decision to make when it came to Cory.

"You're wondering what you should do," Devon said as he leaned on the wall outside the lockers.

"That obvious, eh?" She gave up holding the drinks and set them on the floor.

"Not hard to figure out. The guy appeared out of the blue. Doesn't have the courtesy to even say why he left. Probably the world's biggest douchebag. But the dilemma is, he's Cory's dad."

"No, he's not." The words burst out of her, and she didn't regret them because they were true. "He left."

"Left you. But he didn't know about Cory," Devon replied, playing devil's advocate.

Which was the best thing he could have done because it allowed her to argue and reason out her point. "I don't think it would have mattered. Antoine wasn't the boy I thought I knew."

"So, what will you do?"

She shrugged. "I don't know." A lie. She did know.

She knew the moment she set eyes on the lying bastard. The best course of action involved not mentioning anything to either of them. Cory was doing great without his dad, and Antoine obviously never cared about her. Why rock a perfectly fine boat? Besides the KM agency, the only other entity Tanya felt an obligation to preferred no attachments from the past.

And Antoine was most definitely her past.

A past that should have stayed dead.

The door to the locker room crashed open as the first wave of smelly boys emerged, boisterous, high on their win, and thirsty. There was no more time to talk as Tanya and Devon disbursed drinks, with Cory being one of the last to emerge. Was it wrong to be glad that Devon's bulk hid him from anyone who might be watching through the glass? She wondered if Antoine had left or remained behind. If she ran Cory past him, would it occur to him to look closely and question his parentage? Because Cory looked nothing like Devon.

Her heart still hadn't recovered from the anxiety that Antoine might find out about Cory. She was glad that Devon had been quick enough to cover for her because upon seeing Antoine, she'd panicked.

How to explain that he had a son? How to handle the fact that she wouldn't give him up?

"Did you see the way I got in front of that puck on that breakaway?"

Tanya was startled by her son's exuberant question.

"Dude, that was some smooth skating. When you decked him... Damn," Devon exclaimed, drawing Cory's attention. In that moment, he played the part of the better parent.

"We should get you into a hot shower," Tanya stated. "Then feed you a proper brunch. Your next game is at four."

Exiting the dressing hall, her gaze darted all around, but she saw no sign of Antoine. Not inside the arena or in the parking lot. A tension she'd not truly realized eased.

Devon noticed. He brushed close and whispered by her ear, "Keep it together. Your boy is sharp, and he's watching."

Indeed, he was, from the backseat as he insisted Devon ride in front with Tanya once he found out that Devon had gotten a ride to the arena rather than driving himself. If she didn't know better, she'd suspect the kid of matchmaking. Had he enlisted his *aunts'* aid in trying to set her up? A failed prospect from the get-go, given she would not be dating Devon.

Why not? Today, she'd lost her reason to abstain. She wasn't a widow. Being with another man wouldn't be betraying anyone.

I shouldn't jump in too quickly. She had Cory to think about.

Arriving at the lodge, she was a twitching mess, which might be why Devon held onto her in the hall outside her room while Cory went in for his shower. "Show me how the ice machine works because I cannot figure it out." He tugged her down the hall, and yet she noticed how he kept an eye on her room even once they reached the machine. The hum of it proved loud enough to cover a low conversation. "You need to get your shit together."

"Excuse me if I'm a little shook that my son's daddy just rose from the dead," she snapped.

"Shook is allowed, but sloppy is not. That man is dangerous."

She snorted. "No, duh. Which is why I can't let Antoine see Cory."

"That's not the only reason. The wedding ring wasn't the only thing your dead ex was hiding. He's carrying."

"What are you talking—?" She clued in. "Oh." He meant that Antoine was carrying a weapon. "Are you sure? He never took off his coat."

"Very sure."

Her lips pursed. "He never did say why he was at that arena."

"What else was going on other than the hockey game?"

She rolled her shoulders. "Not much. A bake sale with proceeds going to a concussion charity. The usual buy and sell of used equipment and new gear. I suppose he could have a kid in the tournament." It almost gutted her to say it, mostly because seeing him made her feel stupid. So very, very stupid.

"You look pissed."

"Because I am," she grumbled. "Why did he have to come back now?"

"Why does it matter? Just avoid him until the end of the tournament. And then you never have to see him again."

"Easy for you to say. He is still technically Cory's father."

"He donated sperm. He's not his dad."

"Because he never had a chance." Now, she was the one arguing his case, second-guessing herself.

"Don't start making excuses for the douchebag."

She sighed. "I know. It's just…"

"Suddenly, this guy you put on an impossible pedestal reappears in your life, and not only does it look like he wasn't worthy of your love, he threatens your happiness."

Hearing him put it in words acted as a bludgeon. "He could change everything."

"Only if you let him."

"I don't want to."

"Then don't. You get to decide, Bunny."

"Is that fair to Cory?"

"You're his mother. Isn't part of the job protecting him?"

"I can't believe this is happening." She paced in short, tight circles, rubbing her forehead.

"It's pretty fucked up, I'll give you that. But I'm here, Bunny. Whatever you need, I'll help you."

The sincerity in the words hit Tanya, and she stopped and stared at Devon, noticing his rugged good looks anew. His earnest expression. Her recollection of his honor from six years ago. The way he'd slept in the bed beside her and not taken advantage at all.

The jerk.

The only other man she'd ever even thought about kissing. A man that might help her forget.

She threw herself at Devon, clutching his jacket, yanking him close, almost knocking them both out in her spontaneous decision to kiss him.

But she had to touch him. Needed to remind herself that it wasn't too late for her to live, feel, maybe even love again.

Not that she let any of that spill out. She kept the verbal garbage inside and just kissed him.

And he kissed her back, with his hands cupping her ass, and a low hum of pleasure rumbling from him, vibrating against her mouth.

The heat between them built, and she burned with need. Wanted to explode, only to gasp and redden in embarrassment when her son, sounding much too amused, said, "Are we going to eat, or are you guys sucking face a while longer?"

How bad of a mother would it make her if she told her son to go away?

Instead, she stepped away from Devon, her cheeks

burning hot. In a voice none too steady, she said, "Who's hungry?"

"I am," Devon murmured at her back, almost causing her to stumble.

"I need coffee." And a cold shower, because she had a feeling this would be a long lunch.

CHAPTER ELEVEN

DEVON WANTED TO SKIP LUNCH. After that kiss, no way could he sit across from Tanya and not lust. The woman ignited him in ways he'd never imagined.

The problem was, he doubted she felt the same way about him.

The return of Cory's dad had almost shattered her. And he knew that encounter was the only reason she'd kissed him. What did it say about him that he wished the boy hadn't interrupted?

He shouldn't be taking advantage of her confusion. Then again, a woman who managed to remain celibate for fifteen years was probably more than capable of making her own choices.

And she'd chosen Devon.

The knowledge hummed inside him as he ate, and he spent a good portion of their meal hard, especially since every time he caught her gaze, she blushed and ducked her head. He enjoyed her reaction way too much and wanted to drag her somewhere private to finish that kiss. Which would really make things complicated.

After all, his mission would only last a few days. Then, he'd fly back home. Not exactly fair of him to get involved if he couldn't stick around.

Damn his honor. Rather than act on his desires, he saw Tanya and Cory to their hotel room door after their meal and then claimed he had to run some errands before the boy's next game.

Not exactly a lie. Devon needed to find out more about this Antoine character because his sudden reappearance seemed very suspicious. And, no, it wasn't just jealousy making him look. The guy had come back from the dead. It deserved investigation, especially given the fact that he didn't exist.

Devon had fired off an email to Mason at BBI to do a search for the guy. According to every database Mason searched, Antoine didn't exist. Not alive, at any rate.

Which meant, he'd changed his name. Legally, or not? Either way, given his age and means at the time, he must have had help. Devon set Mason to figuring out who Antoine had become, and while that was going on, he planned to do some work on his actual mission.

Find the guy in charge of the chop shops. Marcel

Lavoie presented as the perfect suspect for his case. A guy with no reason to be here. He wasn't with the hockey teams. Nor did he appear to ski or snowboard. Why stay in a hotel that catered exclusively to that set? There were other places more centrally located for the less skiing-inclined.

And who was his damned roommate?

The kid had said that he wore a suit.

Antoine wore a suit.

That coincidence would be much too huge. Yet it nagged at Devon, which meant he had to find out for sure.

With Marcel having registered under his name alone, Devon had nothing to go on. He would have to resort to stealthier methods, a specialty of his.

Hence why he'd put himself in the stairwell, watching the room marked 305 through a tiny slit in the door. As far as he knew, Marcel and his buddy were inside. Or so he hoped. Could be he watched for nothing.

Keeping an ear out for anyone coming through the stairwell, he faked banality each time a random stair climber appeared. When a couple jogged up the stairs and past him, huffing and puffing, he posed and pretended to be tying his boots. For the man who stomped up the stairs, a glower on his face, Devon feigned interest in his phone. A common activity that people never seemed to question, no matter the strange spot.

During those interruptions, Devon did his best not to lose sight of Marcel's door. It would suck if they exited and Devon didn't notice. The stray mitten he'd snared from the lobby acted as an innocuous doorstop. Just enough to give him a peek.

A master at his craft, he'd long ago learned the art of surveillance and being sneaky. What he apparently needed was a refresher course on the stealthy nature of a teenage ninja in socks who whispered, "Who we spying on?"

Startled by the query and the fact he'd been caught, Devon glanced at Cory, who grinned cheekily.

"Er, I don't know what you're talking about. I'm not spying."

"Then why you got your eye on this floor?" Cory frowned. "Are you stalking someone other than my mom? I thought you had the hots for her."

Devon totally did. But that was not exactly something he'd say aloud to her kid. "Don't worry, I'm not cheating on your mom."

"Better not be." Said with all the growly menace a fourteen-year-old was capable of. "And you still haven't told me why you're spying. You waiting to beat someone up?" Cory's expression looked much too intrigued.

"First off, I would never admit it even if I was. Second, if you're going to beat someone's ass, do it where you won't be seen. You don't want witnesses." Words of wisdom from a guy who'd gotten a dressing-down by his boss because a neighbor had caught Devon tenderizing the flesh of a crime lord who needed to be taught a lesson.

"I don't know how to fight." Cory's nose wrinkled. "I asked Mom about joining a Jujitsu place or even kickboxing, but she said I was too busy with hockey in the winter and baseball in the summer."

"I could teach you." The words slipped out by accident. The thing was, he actually meant it. The kid appeared bright, and he had athletic skill. He was also at the age where he might need to defend himself. The teen years could be rough ones.

"Would you really?" Cory's expression brightened. "Shit, yeah," he exclaimed, then gasped. "Don't tell my mom I said that."

That brought a chuckle to Devon's lips. "It'll be our secret."

"Speaking of secrets, when you gonna tell me why you're watching this floor?"

It actually pained him to say, "It's nothing you need to worry about." The kid deserved the truth. Unfortunately, this was one of those times he had to lie.

"Are you sure you're not here to smack someone around? Because this is the floor that big, bald dick is staying on."

Could Cory be talking about Marcel? "Why is he a dick?"

Cory leaned against the wall in a nonchalant

slouch only the boneless youth could achieve. A hank of hair flopped over his forehead. "My buddy Shane is on this floor, and he said when he tried to get on the elevator, even though it was empty, the jerk shoved him aside and told him to get on the next."

"Did Shane say if he had someone with him?"

"Yeah. Some dude in a suit." Cory stared at him. "Are they some kind of criminals? Are you like a cop or something, staking them out?"

"Let's go with 'or something.'" Tanya probably wouldn't appreciate Devon telling her kid that he worked as a problem-solving kind of guy.

"You got a gun?"

Devon hedged before admitting anything. "Yeah. A few." He didn't mention the one in his ankle holster, the only spot that people truly didn't notice, which was important in a province that didn't allow the carrying of them in public.

"My mom has guns, too."

The remark threw him for a loop. "She told you?"

"What?" Cory laughed. "No way. She'd probably freak if she knew I found her stashes."

"How many stashes?" Devon asked.

"Let's see." Cory ticked off the list using his fingers. "Inside the front hall drawer in that fancy dresser thing. In the bathroom, under the sink. The laundry room has one in a basket of lonely socks. She's got a few in her bedroom and the kitchen. And there's a rifle strapped under the couch."

"Um." Devon had no words.

"I'm pretty sure she has more. But those are the ones I've found so far. It's like a Where's Waldo game." Cory smiled. "The first time I came across one, I thought my mom might be some kind of secret spy or something."

"Your mom?" Devon laughed and hoped the kid didn't hear the falsity in it.

"Yeah, crazy, right?" Cory snickered. "I mean, she's my mom."

Devon felt a need to speak. "She's pretty amazing."

"Good answer or I'd have to kick your butt." The kid smiled again, and Devon couldn't help but respond in kind.

"So, you never said what you were up to. What happened to resting before your game?" Devon asked.

The kid's nose wrinkled. "Snuck out for some air because mom is in crazy mode."

"Crazy how?"

Cory shrugged. "Went in the bedroom and jumped on her computer."

"Probably catching up on work."

"Maybe. When she gets like that, she claims she's got some kind of decorating emergency with a client."

"Interior design can be an intense thing. I work in real estate." Might as well stick to the partial truth. Because Devon did work as a realtor in between his other jobs.

"How intense can choosing colors be?" Cory rolled his eyes. "Anyhow, she's in the zone, and I was bored."

"Does she know you left?"

"Yeah. Told me not to talk to strangers." A moue accompanied the statement.

"Sounds like normal motherly advice."

"For a baby."

The teen was much too bright and inquisitive for his own good. "Maybe she's stressed about something going on with work."

"Maybe you should go see her and help her to relax," Cory said quite innocently. "I'll be gone at least forty minutes, probably closer to an hour."

Devon blinked. Had the kid just tried to hook him up with his mom? "Um. Er. I can't."

"Because of the spying thing." Cory nodded. "Gotcha. By the way, they're leaving."

"What?" He spun to look and watched the bulky shape of Marcel following that of a man in a wool trench coat. The style of it was familiar. Could it be...?

"Gotcha," Cory whispered.

Hard to deny his interest now. But how to ditch Cory so he could get into that room. He pretended disinterest in the hall. "So, your mom is alone, eh? Maybe I'll pay her a visit."

It killed him to turn his back on the hall and the kid. What if Marcel and his companion turned around and came right back. He'd never know. But he had to ditch the teen.

Devon headed down the stairs to the second floor. Cory skipped past him, grinning the entire time. "Later."

"Yeah," Devon muttered as he entered the second floor and pretended to head up the hall. Counting in his head how long it would take Cory to make it to the main level. He gave it an extra ten seconds then returned to the stairwell and took the stairs two at a time. He hit the third level and—

—couldn't avoid Cory grinning at him. "I knew it."

"What are you doing here?" Devon grumbled.

"Keeping an eye. You'll be glad to know the dick is still gone. Which means I can keep watch while you toss the place."

There was no point in lying. "How does you watching help me? How would you warn me they're coming?"

"I'll stand at the corner and watch the elevator. If I see them in it, I'll race back and warn you by knocking on the wall."

Say no. Say no. "Only if you promise that after you warn me, you keep on running. I don't want either Marcel or his friend to see you."

"Don't worry. I'll be like the wind." Cory grinned, the fearlessness of youth in his face.

The lump in Devon's gut indicated that not only was this probably a dumb idea but that Tanya would freak if she heard about it.

But the kid did offer, and really, the danger was

more on Devon because he was the one doing the actual searching. If he got caught in someone's room? He'd be in trouble for sure. Nothing he couldn't handle, but it would blow his cover.

Therefore, a warning giving him time to get out would help. And, quite honestly, chances were that Marcel and company would be gone for at least fifteen minutes. It took that long just to get a coffee from the shop on the main floor. "One knock, and you run. Promise?"

"Heck, yeah." Cory fist-pumped.

"Let's go. Quietly, now. We don't want people in their rooms hearing us." Devon went through the stairwell door.

"How you gonna get in?" Cory stage-whispered by Devon's side as they headed for their target room.

"Special app." Devon waggled his phone. He already had the lock app loaded. It would act as a keycard when tapped against the door pad.

Click. The door unlocked.

"Epic!" Cory breathed.

"Keep watch," Devon admonished before the kid changed his mind and tried to follow him in.

"On it." Cory jogged down the hall to the corner where he could see the elevator.

Which did nothing for the stairwell. Here was hoping Marcel's companion wasn't the type to want to hit the stairs for exercise.

Entering the suite, Devon noticed that it had the

same layout as Tanya's, including the couch done up with sheets and a pillow. So, the men definitely weren't sleeping together.

He ignored the bathroom and even the living room suite area to enter the bedroom. The bed was sloppily made, indicating that housekeeping hadn't been by.

The question was, would someone be comfortable that their space would remain undisturbed, even with such orders given? A quick glance around showed nothing overtly on display. Which was why Devon went for the electronic safe in the closet first—and noticed the suits hanging neatly.

Nice suits. Two of them in total.

Lots of guys wore suits.

Devon spent a short moment loading a different app, this one designed to bypass the need for a code on hotel safes. People were so gullible to believe those electronic boxes were any good. It gave a false sense of security. In reality, anyone could easily open them.

Click. The door popped open, and there was nothing inside. A true let-down.

Devon slammed it shut and whirled to look at what else was in the room. A suitcase sat zippered on the floor. Devon dropped to his knees, flipped it over, and noticed the lock holding the zipper tabs shut.

His phone didn't have an app for that one, but he did have a specialized keychain with TSA knockoff keys. He thumbed through his strange collection, the keys themselves camouflaged to look like other things.

It took the third one before he popped the lock. The *rrr* sound as he pulled the zippers open screamed in the quiet room.

Rushing wasn't ideal, but Devon couldn't be sure if he'd have a minute or an hour to properly search.

The suitcase held only a few articles of clothing, no surprise. A quick riffle showed nothing evident. So, he dumped out the left half and undid the zipper liner. A hand around the inside showed nothing out of place. He put the clothes back, trying to keep the layout the same, probably failing. He could only hope that they wouldn't notice. He emptied the other side and undid the zipper liner. This time, he touched an envelope. He withdrew the brown manila, but before he could deal with the sealed edge, he heard it: a brisk knock.

Shit. No time to be fancy. He shoved the clothes back, slammed the suitcase shut, and started yanking the zipper, wasting time. The lock refused to click.

So be it. He shoved the envelope into his pants, set the suitcase upright, and then moved quickly to the door, expecting it to open at any moment.

It didn't, hence why—ready for a confrontation— he stepped out. No one stood in the hall either, but he did hear voices.

"...know if the gift shop sells glass moose?"

"Fuck off," snapped the distinctive voice of Marcel.

"Dude. Chill."

"The boy is right, chill." Spoken by a stranger with

some amusement. "Why don't you go fetch the car while I grab what I forgot."

"He work for you?" Cory asked.

"Marcel? Yes. I rarely travel without assistance."

"Why?"

"Because. I am here for business."

"What kind of business?" Cory nosily asked, and Devon could have groaned. The kid was playing a dangerous game.

"I am acquiring something of worth. Why do you need a glass moose?" The more the guy spoke, the more Devon thought he knew the voice. That accent.

Oh, shit.

"Promised my girlfriend I'd get her something."

The kid was good, Devon would give him that. But he was even better. He came around the corner, confirmed his suspicion, and exclaimed, "There you are. I thought you were supposed to be taking it easy. You've got a big game this afternoon, *son.*" Would Cory get the reference?

The kid glanced at him over his shoulder. "Hey, Dad." A fake name, and yet Devon enjoyed it. "I know I'm supposed to take it easy, but I was going stir-crazy. So, I popped down to see Shane, but he's actually having a nap like a little kid, so I thought I'd get Cherise something."

"I told you already, you are way too young to be getting serious about a girl," Devon grumbled.

"Nothing wrong with young love," said Antoine,

the hint of a smirk on his lips. At least Marcel had left. A bit of luck, given the man could have completely shredded Devon's charade. He needed to get Cory out of here before Antoine noticed anything amiss.

"Sorry my boy bugged you. We'll get going." Devon clapped a hand on Cory's shoulder.

"A pleasure to meet your *son*." Antoine stared at Devon, and yet he still got a chill.

"Who are you?" Cory asked, with the bluntness of youth.

Could it be so simple? Would Antoine give his name?

"I'd better get going before my companion returns with an even fouler disposition."

"We'll get out of your way then." Devon moved them towards the elevator.

"I hope you find what you're looking for," called out Antoine.

"Did you?" Cory whispered once the doors closed. "Find anything that is."

"Nope." He lied because whatever was in his back pocket probably wasn't for the kid's eyes. The doors opened on to the main floor, but when Cory would have walked off in the direction of the lounge, Devon reeled him back. "Wrong way."

"Where are we going?" the kid asked.

"Gift shop, just in case they decide to come down and check out your story."

"You think they will?" Cory glanced over his shoulder, about as discreet as an elephant in short grass.

"Maybe.

The kid truly had a bright smile. "Cool."

If only Devon had his enthusiasm. He remained all too aware of the envelope tucked down the back of his pants, under his shirt. Knew he'd fucked up given the boy and Antoine had met. Would probably regret it.

"Who are they anyhow?"

A loaded question. One Devon wasn't about to answer. "Hey, look, they've got a glass beaver in the window!"

The distraction worked. For now. But Devon worried about what would happen when the kid invariably slipped up with his mom.

She'd kill Devon. Probably string him up by the heels and eviscerate him.

In his defense, he had no way of knowing that Marcel and Antoine were together, a suspicion yes, but only because he hated the guy and wanted him to be up to no good so he could shoot him.

The good news? Marcel didn't blow Devon's cover.

Going against him? The fact that he'd involved Cory in the first place, which might be why he felt guilty enough to bring treats when he escorted Cory back to his room.

The ridiculous price tag proved totally worth the smile on Tanya's face when he showed up with a travel cup of hot cocoa.

"Oooh, it has whipped cream."

Watching her lick the foamy top was the best thing to happen to him since the kiss.

The worst?

Cory's announced. "Hey, so now that you and Devon are a couple, does this mean I might get a baby sister?"

"Um. Er." Tanya gaped like a fish.

Devon, sucker-punched as well, managed a platitude. "Too soon to be talking about things like that."

"No! The answer is no," Tanya exclaimed, her cheeks sporting two bright red spots. "Devon, can I speak with you?"

Tanya waited until she'd shut the bedroom door before hitting Devon. Quite a few times, actually.

"Oh my God, why does Cory think you're going to impregnate me? What did you say to him?"

He'd said a few things such as, "Don't tell your mom" and "I hope if you have a girlfriend, you're using rubbers."

To which he was relieved to hear, "Gross, dude. We're not even fifteen yet!"

"I didn't say anything," Devon exclaimed, grabbing her hands.

She scowled up at him. "Then why the sudden weird interest?"

"Maybe he really wants a sister," he said in a squeaky voice. As if he could help it. He'd never thought about having kids before, and now that Cory had tossed that grenade out there, he couldn't *stop* thinking of it.

What would it be like to have a child of his own? Someone to teach? And love? And protect?

Ah, shit.

"I blame you for this," Tanya hissed. "How did you run into each other anyhow?"

Admitting that the boy had run surveillance while Devon stole from her ex-boyfriend probably wasn't the brightest idea, which meant the envelope stayed tucked in his pants. "Gift shop. He was browsing around for a present, and I helped him out."

"A gift for who?"

"His girlfriend."

Her lips pursed. "He is entirely way too serious about her for this age."

"I agree."

That got him a look. "What about the hot chocolate?"

"His suggestion. Apparently, you have a weakness for sweets."

"That's not the only thing," she muttered, staring at his mouth.

Only one thing to do. Devon leaned in for a kiss.

CHAPTER TWELVE

TANYA DODGED out of Devon's reach before his lips could land. Not because she didn't want a kiss. The problem was more that she craved one.

And he knew it, too.

Devon didn't chase after her. Just tucked his hands behind his back, the hint of a grin on his lips.

She wagged a finger. "No more kisses."

"Why not?"

"Because."

"Am I a bad kisser?"

"No." Only as she said it, did she realize that she should have lied.

"Then why won't you kiss me? And don't you dare use your ex as an excuse. He's not dead. And he's married."

The reminder pulled her lips down. "I know. That's not why we shouldn't be making out."

"Give me a good reason."

"We're colleagues."

"Who work out of different offices.

"For competing companies," she noted.

"Collaboration isn't unheard of."

"You're leaving in a few days."

"Do you want commitment?"

Her lips flattened. "No." And at the same time, yes. She'd spent the last fifteen years alone. It would be nice to have someone to share life with.

"You're attracted to me."

"Yes." Again, she just couldn't lie. "But we can't do anything about it. Or have you forgotten Cory's in the other room."

That brought a slow smile. "Cory just asked us to make a baby. I'm pretty sure that means he's okay with me giving you a smooch."

"Except you won't stop at a kiss," she huffed. The other problem was she wouldn't try to stop him either. She wanted that and more.

"Can I help it if you turn me on?" Said with a shrug.

"You need to focus on our case. I found out some interesting stuff while you were out shopping." She sat cross-legged on her bed, yanking the computer into her lap. A chastity belt of sorts.

Making himself at home, he sprawled alongside her. "Hit me."

"I did," she teased. "So, turns out that Marcel guy we're interested in has a bit of a rap sheet."

"How did Mason miss it?"

"Because it happened when he was a juvenile, so the records are sealed."

"Not to you."

She smirked. "I have my ways."

"What was he charged with?"

"Mostly death threats and assault."

"Big surprise."

"Nothing severe enough to serve jail time, but lots of probation, a few stints in juvie, and plea deals for community service."

"So not a nice boy. But is the man still a thug?"

"Probably, but he hasn't done anything that's gotten him arrested."

"Who's he work for?"

"That was a tougher nut to crack," she admitted. "Turns out, he's employed by a security firm."

"Bodyguard for hire?"

"Apparently. So, I hacked their company records."

"Not a very good security firm," he noted.

She couldn't help but look pleased as she said, "Their protection was good. Just not as good as me."

"What did you discover, oh hacker extraordinaire?"

"That this company only does full-time work a for a few people. One of them is Madam Gisele Boucher, a high-end jewelry designer with a shop in Montreal. A Frederick Agneaux, who is a government official. And a Jean-Guy Lapierre, who is registered as an import-export kind of guy."

Devon scrubbed at his jaw, showing signs of bristle. "So, in the interest of sharing info, I guess I should mention that Antoine is Marcel's roommate."

"What? Are you sure? How did you find out?"

"I saw them together."

"Here? In the lodge?" Her eyes widened. "Shit. I need to leave."

"If you're freaking about Cory, stop. Antoine doesn't know you have a kid. And if he sees one with you, he'll assume Cory's mine. Like we told him."

"Except Cory looks nothing like you."

"Or you," he pointed out.

Her lips flattened. "We should go before he figures it out."

"Leave before the tournament is done? Not very subtle." Devon arched a brow. "How you going to explain it to your kid?"

"I'll tell him there was an emergency back home."

"What if he asks to stay with one of his buddies?"

She couldn't help but glare at Devon as he poked holes in her plan. "What do you suggest I do?"

"As I see it, we have a few options. One, you tell Antoine that Cory's his kid."

"Never." Tanya wasn't budging on that point.

"Two, act casual, finish the tournament, and go home with no one the wiser."

"That's your brilliant plan?"

"Actually, there is a third option. We find out what Antoine and Marcel are up to and nail their asses to a wall."

"Because you think Antoine's a criminal."

"Look who he's associating with."

"I wouldn't judge. Look at who I'm hanging with?" Tanya retorted hotly.

"Admit it, you're having fun." He winked then turned serious. "You weren't the only one digging. I had Mason poking around, too. Antoine doesn't exist."

"Obviously, or I would have found him before this." She rolled her eyes. "He must have changed his name."

"He'd have to since he died. The question remains, why?" Devon asked.

"I don't know." But she'd been asking herself that same thing since she saw him. The shock of it still had her inwardly quivering. When the accident first happened, she used to imagine that he'd somehow survived and would come searching for her. And when she saw him, she'd cry and then throw her arms around his neck, and they'd live happily ever after.

The reality? The sight of him had filled her with chilling fear and hot rage.

She'd obviously never meant as much to him as she'd believed. And she'd damned well die before she let Cory find out what an asshole his father was.

She began ticking off her fingers. "People change identities for a few reasons: finances,"—money being a strong driver of questionable decisions—"and scandal."

"What kind of scandal? He left before he knew you were pregnant. Was he about to be arrested?"

A good question. "I don't think so. You'd think if he was worried, he'd have been scared to run into someone from his past."

"He didn't look too worried when he saw you."

She tapped her chin. "In retrospect, he didn't appear surprised at all. Leading me to believe he doesn't care if people know he's alive anymore."

"Which leaves money as a possible reason," Devon observed. "Why would someone pay him to leave, though?"

Tanya shrugged. "Or there's another reason we're not seeing. Maybe he suddenly decided he'd had enough of small-town life and thought the only way to branch off was to"—fake his death and abandon his girlfriend—"leave everything and start over."

"Could be he witnessed a crime and worried about someone coming after him."

"Maybe he did go through the ice and was suffering from amnesia. And by the time he recovered, years had passed, and he had a new life."

Devon stared at her.

She shrugged. "It happens."

"In movies," he said with a snort. "Given your ex is here with Marcel, I'm going to say he's involved in something hinky. Think we can match him up to one of those names you got from the security firm?"

She drummed her fingers on the smooth part of her laptop. "Possibly. I hadn't gotten that far yet. A quick Internet search showed no images for Agneaux or Lapierre."

"And Gisele?"

The corner of her lip quirked. "I saw pics, and it's not Antoine. Could be Marcel isn't here for work at all. Maybe he's having a getaway with his lover."

"They are not gay."

"You can't be sure."

"You dated Antoine. Had sex with him."

"People change," she stated, doing her best to not wonder if that was why he'd left her.

"He's not gay. His bodyguard sleeps on the couch."

Her gaze narrowed. "How do you know that?"

Rather than explain, he exclaimed, "Shit. Doesn't Cory have to be at the arena in like fifteen minutes?"

Devon no sooner spoke than there was a knock at the door. "Hey, are we heading over to the arena together or should I hitch another ride?"

"I'm coming," Tanya yelled. Then in a softer aside said, "We're not done yet."

"I should hope not." Devon winked. That simple gesture shouldn't have had the power to heat her insides like a marshmallow over flames.

"You grabbing a ride with me?"

"Sure."

Devon completely ignored her on the ride over to the arena in order to grill her son about the team they were playing. They talked stats and numbers while she mulled over what she'd learned thus far. Which wasn't much.

Antoine, who wasn't Antoine, was here with a petty criminal for some unknown reason. But more and more, she had to wonder if they were Devon's target. Their shadiness fit the bill. How to be sure, though?

If only she could pinpoint their phones in the data signal mess she was still sorting through. Once she located them and cracked their devices, she'd know for sure. Was Antoine crooked? Did he suspect her secret? Was he actually married? And for how long?

Because a small part of her remained hurt. Hurt and wondering how long it had been before Antoine forgot the girl he'd told lies to.

At the arena, she chose to sit inside, parking her butt on a cold bench, clapping her mittened hands at every good play.

Devon sat beside her, his solid frame close enough to hers that their thighs brushed—which gave her a ridiculous thrill. His enthusiasm caused her heart to hammer. The times he glanced at her? A spurt of heat between her legs dampened her panties.

In the third period, when Devon's phone rang and he left to take the call, disappointment filled her. She'd not expected how much enjoyment she'd feel at having someone by her side.

Apparently, that applied only to a specific person, and that someone wasn't Antoine. He arrived suddenly, dressed once more in a suit and trench more suitable for wintery weather downtown than a cold hockey arena. Without asking permission, he took Devon's place on the bench. Too close for her comfort, but she didn't shift and show him her annoyance. She had to watch what she did and said very carefully.

Because his son was on the ice.

My son. Which meant she had to protect him, especially from this stranger who'd suddenly appeared in her life.

"Why are you here again?" she snapped.

"I am a big lover of amateur sports."

"Since when?" Her lip curled. She remembered all too well his disdain for the jocks of the world.

Rather than reply, he took another tack. "It's really nice of you to show support for your boyfriend's child."

Tanya tried to appear relaxed. "Not hard at all. He's a good kid." The best, which was why he didn't deserve having his life and mental state shaken upside down by Antoine—or whatever the heck he was calling himself now.

"I'm surprised you don't have any kids of your own. You always talked about having a few."

What the hell was this small talk? "Never met the right guy." Or it could be she had, but she'd been so caught up in her guilt that she'd never acted on it.

No more.

"Pity, you'd make a great mother. You always did have a caring streak."

"You're right, I did. Ask me how long I cried after I thought you died?" She turned to fix Antoine with a glare. Time to move from being on the defensive to making him answer some questions.

"Unfortunate but necessary. I had to make a clean break."

"Unfortunate?" She almost choked on the word. "You made everyone think you were dead. Your parents. Friends. Me. It was cruel."

"You got over it and moved on."

The fact that she hadn't was a shameful secret she wouldn't reveal. "Are you ever going to tell me why?"

"Is there any point? What's done is done."

His refusal to answer only heightened her irritation. "What have you been doing all this time?"

"This and that."

As vague as he could get. "Where?"

"Why the interest? It's not as if we'll see each other again. Or are you trying to tell me something?" Antoine asked, his eyes and face a more mature version of the boy she'd once loved. Familiar and yet utterly alien.

And was it her, or did she detect something cold and calculating in his gaze? Had it always been there?

"If you're asking if I want to rekindle things, then the answer is no."

"Are you sure, *ma belle*?" He used the French nickname for her that she'd not heard in fifteen years. Once upon a time, it had given her flutters. Now, she wanted to slap him in the face.

"Very sure."

"Would it help if I said I did miss you?" He placed his hand on her leg, and she looked at it, feeling nothing. Actually, that wasn't true. Rage simmered inside. Did he think her so stupid?

Pushing his arm away, she drawled, "You missed me so much you never once called."

"And what would I have said? A clean break was better for us both."

"Better for you, maybe. It was an awful thing to do, and you know it."

He leaned back. "You don't seem to be suffering."

"You prick," she snarled. "Your arrogance is outstanding. I don't know how your wife handles it."

Antoine glanced down at his hand with the ring as glaring evidence. "Isabella appreciates a man of substance."

"Does she know you're a liar?"

His lips quirked, but his eyes didn't hold any hint of a smile. "Isabella knows what's good for her."

The statement was enough to make her realize she was doing the right thing by keeping Cory a secret, and she needed to get away from Antoine. "I'd say it was nice seeing you, but it wasn't. You are right. You dying was probably the best thing you could have done for me. Have a good life." She stood as the final buzzer sounded, and Cory's team won.

"So much fire. A far cry from the shy girl I used to know." Antoine stood, too, and she noticed he was only a little taller than she was. Definitely not anywhere near as tall as Devon.

"You mean the pushover?" She snorted. "Bye, Antoine."

"Have dinner with me?" he said, not taking the hint.

"Why?" she asked over her shoulder.

"Perhaps because seeing you again has reminded me of what I left behind."

"And I told you, not interested."

"Then give me a chance to say I'm sorry."

He said all the right things, yet there was no apology in his tone, and almost a mockery in his expression.

"I don't think so." She went to move past, but he grabbed her by the arm.

"Are you sure? Because it feels as if there is unfinished business between us."

Looking at Antoine, a man for whom she'd put her life on hold for fifteen years, she could say with some relief, "No. There's not."

But rather than let her escape, Antoine drew closer. "You say no, and yet, as I recall, all it took was a kiss to change your mind." He leaned in, and she felt a fluttery panic as his mouth approached.

Excuse me? Hell, no.

The shove might have been harder than warranted given he stumbled and almost fell down the bleachers. Tanya didn't care. Her cheeks flamed hotly as she declared, "I am not interested."

"We'll see about that." Antoine gathered himself and left, the squaring of his shoulders tense.

And, for some reason, she had an urge to flee. Just grab Cory and run because a bad feeling brought a sour taste to her mouth, one that hinted of fear.

CHAPTER THIRTEEN

DEVON TOOK some pleasure in seeing Tanya avoiding the wandering lips of her ex-lover. And, no, it wasn't creepy that he watched.

He only wished he could have heard the conversation between them. It appeared intense, but given that Antoine's face creased in anger as he left, Devon could guess what had happened.

Rejected!

He felt elated more than he probably should. What did he care if Tanya hooked up with another dude? He wasn't all that interested in her... Aw, fuck. Who was he kidding? He climbed up the bleachers and met her coming across.

"Hey, Bunny. The boys won!"

"They did. And you can stop pretending. I know you saw me with company," Tanya said with a scowl.

"What did he want?"

"Apparently, to give me some BS about how he had to leave and make me think he was dead, then thought he could just step back into my life and bed."

"And your answer to that was?"

The look she gave him might have withered a less confident man. "What do you think I said?"

He grinned. "To stuff it where the sun don't shine?"

Her expression softened. "More or less. You were right, he is married. Some poor woman named Isabella."

"Did you ask him if he took a new name?"

She shook her head. "No. Dammit. He had me so damned mad, I didn't even think to ask. But the good news is he still thinks Cory is yours, and we should keep it that way."

"No urge to introduce the kid to his daddy?" Devon prodded gently.

Might as well have poked a hornet's nest with a stick. "That man is not his father," Tanya spat.

And then, because he apparently had a moron gene, Devon asked, "Is it fair, though, not to tell him?"

"None of your damned business."

"Probably not. But as a child who grew up with a mother who tossed his dad out when I was just a little boy, I can say meeting his father is probably something Cory's always dreamed about."

Tanya halted and turned to hiss at him. "So, I should explain to my son how his father abandoned me and him? How he let me think he was dead? How he went on with his life with no care for the damage he did? That he even remarried, maybe had kids?"

Much as he knew it would get him in trouble, Devon muttered, "You know, when I first found out he was alive, I was thinking like you, that it was best if you kept him and Cory apart."

"I hear a but."

Devon shrugged. "Maybe you should tell Antoine, or if not him, then Cory at least. Let him make the choice." Let the boy discover that his father was an asshole on his own.

She whirled with a snort. "He's just a kid."

"He's also a smart dude."

"As if you'd know what's right for my kid."

"You're reacting out of anger."

"Damned right, I am. What good could possibly come out of him meeting Antoine? The guy is a sleaze."

"Yeah. He is. But Cory doesn't know that. As a matter of fact, I'll bet your kid currently has his dad on a pedestal. Thinks he's a hero that can do no wrong."

"Cory thinks Antoine is dead."

"Doesn't mean the boy has no feelings about the man. Take it from someone who grew up without a father. I spent a good portion of my childhood thinking I didn't live up to my dad's standards. See, I didn't remember him. I just knew his name and the fact that Mom never spoke of him. In my mind, he became some impossibly mighty being who must have left because I did something bad."

"You said your mom tossed him out? Obviously, there was a reason."

"There was. My dad was a drunk, so as a child, I asked myself, why was he a drunk? Was it because I failed at being a good son?"

She gaped at him. "How could you think that?"

"Because I was a kid missing a father figure, trying to find a reason why mine left."

"Cory's situation is different. He never met his dad. Everyone thinks he's dead."

"But he's not. And much as you want to hide the truth about Antoine, what if you can't? What if Antoine somehow finds out about Cory?"

"He won't."

"Wishful thinking." Devon arched a brow.

"He has no reason to suspect Cory even exists."

"I think you're taking a chance. What if Cory finds out?"

Her lips pressed into a flat line. "I am not telling Skee."

"Why?"

"Because Antoine's a slimeball."

"Is he? Let's be honest, neither of us knows anything about him."

"I know enough. He's not the right kind of person to be in Cory's life."

"Would you like me to kill him then?"

"Yes!" she shouted, only to shake her head. "No."

"Why not? If you don't want Cory to know about him, then killing him is the only way to ensure they never meet."

Her lips trembled, and he hated himself for poking at her logic, but surely she understood that she couldn't just walk away from the truth. "You can't kill him."

"Why not?" Rather than wait, he answered for her. "Because he's Cory's dad."

"He's not. Not in any way that counts," Tanya railed. "Why does he have to be alive? We were doing great without him."

Not really given she refused to move on. "And you'll still do great."

"Only if Cory doesn't find out."

"You're afraid," he stated. Afraid that Cory would blame her for his father leaving. That her son would abandon her, too.

"What if," she whispered, "he tries to take Cory from me?"

"That boy adores you."

"Because he only has me. What if you're right, though? What if he misses having a dad and suddenly sees Antoine and decides he'd rather live with him?"

The anguish just about crushed him. Devon gathered Tanya close, and she didn't fight to move away. He whispered, "Cory would never leave you."

"How can you say that with certainty?" she said, her voice quavering. "After all, Antoine left me. Even my own family threw me out. If Cory goes to be with his father, I'll be alone."

Hugging her even closer, he couldn't help saying, "You don't have to be."

"Are you suggesting yourself as a replacement?" She snorted as she shoved out of his embrace. "You'll be gone in a few days."

A fact he'd tried not to dwell on and didn't like that she'd pointed out. Once he finished this mission, he'd have no reason to stick around.

Nothing except a cute blonde who made him feel... like he belonged with her.

She stalked off muttering, "I need coffee."

He caught up to her. "I'm sorry."

"For what?"

"Butting my nose in. What you do with Cory is none of my business." Yet. He'd not earned a right to have a say, but she was wrong about one thing. He wasn't sure he wanted to leave.

"Damned right, it's not. You have no idea what it's like to be a parent."

"You're right I don't." Yet, oddly, he wanted to find out. "Can I take you and Cory to dinner?"

"It's team dinner night."

"Meaning?"

"The hockey team and parents all eat together. Which means an ungodly wait for food since they try to bring out thirty meals at once."

"Okay. What time is it happening?"

She blinked at him. "Are you insane? Why would you subject yourself to that?"

"Because what if Antoine shows up at the restaurant and sees only you there? It might blow our cover with Cory." The reason he used, the one he knew would work with her rather than the true one. He didn't want to leave her side.

Her lips pressed tight. "Maybe we should skip."

"How would you explain that to Cory?"

In the end, they went to dinner together. Tanya was squished beside Devon at the crammed table, their legs constantly touching as they shared a plate of fries.

And Cory beamed at them from across the table.

Tanya frowned at her son. "Why are you grinning?"

"No reason. Just happy. Are you happy, Mom?" The kid lacked subtlety.

Devon tried to not choke.

"Fine."

"Do you and Devon have plans tonight?" Cory asked.

"I was going to work."

"I was thinking of hitting the slopes for a night ski," Devon said at the same time.

Cory eyed them both, a slight frown between his brows. "Why aren't you doing something together?"

Good question, because a real couple would be hanging out. Devon fabricated a reason. "Your mom thought you'd want a quiet evening before the game tomorrow."

"Oh," was all the boy said on that subject until they were in the elevator later after dinner. Then he put his not-so-subtle teen plan into motion. "Hey, just so you know, I'm going to hang out with Shane and watch a movie. A long one. Which means, I should probably sleep over."

"You can't both sleep on a couch together. It's too small," Tanya replied.

"His mom already ordered a cot for his sister, but she is sleeping over with Gini."

"You have a game tomorrow. You need to be well rested."

Devon almost laughed as Tanya looked for reasons to have her son as a buffer.

"The game isn't until noon. I'll be fine. See you at breakfast." He winked and waved goodbye as they disembarked without him on the second floor.

Because Shane was on the third floor, with Marcel and Antoine. Devon eyed the moving elevator.

"What's wrong?" Tanya asked.

"Maybe I should go with him and make sure he makes it okay."

"Why wouldn't he?" she asked.

He flattened his lips. "Don't freak out."

"Why would I freak out?" she asked.

"Because Shane's room is next door to Marcel and Antoine."

"What?" she squeaked. Her heart raced. "Why didn't you tell me? Shit. We have to stop him. Antoine can't see him."

"Too late. They've already met."

CHAPTER FOURTEEN

THE ANNOUNCEMENT MADE her blood run cold.

"What do you mean they've met?" Tanya eyed him, but Devon couldn't meet her gaze.

"I mean Cory ran into Antoine already."

"And you know this how?"

"Because I was kind of there."

Given the way Devon kept staring at the floor, Tanya knew there was more to it. "You better start talking and hope I like your answers, or you'll be meeting my gun." She jabbed the elevator button, and it must have been on the descent because it opened right away.

She entered and said nothing as he followed. She hit the number three and waited for the doors to close. "Well, I'm still waiting."

"I didn't do it on purpose. I thought I was being

discreet, but your kid caught me watching Marcel's room and then offered to be a lookout."

"To which you said no." Except, judging by his expression, he'd done the opposite. "You idiot! What on Earth made you think that was a good idea?"

"I said no. Even tried to pretend I was coming to see you, but the kid didn't buy it. He ambushed me."

"You're going to blame your lack of skills on a four-teen-year-old boy?"

"With a brilliant mother."

"Don't you try and suck up to me, mister! You put him in danger." The doors slid open, and she stepped out, quick-marching up the hall.

He hurried to stay close, whispering, "I didn't do it intentionally. He was supposed to run if he saw them coming, not have a conversation. If it's any consolation, your boy played along with the being my kid routine."

"Not helping your case."

"What was I supposed to do? I needed to get into Marcel's room."

"I'm sure you could have found another way." They turned the corner, the dreaded room 305 up ahead, no one in the hall.

"You and I both know opportunities can be hard to find."

"I do know." But as a mother, she never would have put her kid in danger.

"Which room is Shane's?" she asked.

Devon pointed at 306. Before Tanya could knock,

she heard masculine laughter that cracked. Her chest eased as she heard Cory's voice.

He was safe.

She marched past right to the stairwell, staying silent as she and Devon skipped down the stairs, not saying a word until the door to her room was shut.

Then she whirled and glared. "How dare you use my son!"

"I'm sorry." He appeared truly contrite. "It won't happen again."

"Damned right, it won't. You need to leave."

"Now?" He nodded. "Of course. I'll just grab my stuff."

He didn't even argue. Just went to the bedroom. For some reason, it infuriated her.

"That's it? You're just going to go? How will you finish your mission?"

"I'll see if they have another room available."

"And if they don't?"

He rolled his shoulders. "I'll figure something out. I won't put you and Cory in danger. I promise."

The very fact that he acquiesced meant she sighed and said, "Don't go."

"But..." He turned a confused expression on her.

"Fact of the matter is, Cory is too smart for his own good. I'm pretty sure he suspects I'm more than just an interior designer."

"He knows about your gun stashes."

"What?" Her lips parted on a startled gasp.

"Even thought his mom was a spy for a while."

"He did?" She blinked at Devon. "How do you know this?"

"He told me."

"He told you," she repeated, sitting on the bed. "He never said anything to me."

"That's because you're his mom."

"Exactly. Yet Cory told you, an almost stranger."

"Ah, but I'm not exactly a stranger to him anymore. I'm dating his mom."

"Fake dating."

"He doesn't know that."

"We have to tell him the truth," she said suddenly. Because it wasn't fair to raise Cory's hopes when this fake courtship would end in a few days.

"What is the truth exactly?"

"That we're only pretending to be a couple."

"What if we weren't?"

"Weren't what?"

"Faking it. I like you, Bunny. A lot."

The fact that he'd said it aloud meant she couldn't ignore it. But she tried. "You really should be concentrating on your case."

A hint of a smile curved his lips. "If you say so. Problem is, I've got nothing. And the office hasn't managed to find extra details either. Any breakthroughs on the signals you hacked?"

"No." She hated to admit that she found herself stymied. None of the phones and laptops she'd managed to hack into appeared to belong to Marcel or Antoine. Which made no sense. Everyone, especially a man who wore a suit and required his own security, had a cell phone, laptop, something with a signal.

"What about you? Did you find anything in Antoine's room?" she asked.

"An envelope hidden in his suitcase."

"What did it contain?"

"I don't know. Cory gave me the signal, and I had to run."

"Pity. That envelope might have had a clue."

"You're right, it might, which is why I brought it with me." He whipped out the envelope, and she ogled it before exploding.

"You stole it!"

"What else was I supposed to do?"

She paced. "He'll know someone is onto him."

Devon rolled his eyes. "A guy into crooked shit always has someone onto him."

"If he's crooked," she defended. "We have only conjecture at his point." And how much of it was colored by her past with Antoine?

His turn to snort. "Seriously? Come on, a dead man resurfaces with a bodyguard in the exact location we were sent to check out. Maybe you want to believe Cory's daddy's hands are clean, but I smell a crook."

"You just don't like him."

"Do you?" he asked, his expression intent.

Her nose wrinkled. "No."

"Good. Then you won't mind if I do this." He dragged her close and kissed her.

It took her by surprise and didn't. The chemistry between them was unmistakable and most definitely wanted. Since she'd met him, she'd been trying to build a shield against his allure, yet Devon kept finding chinks in her armor. And a part of her wanted to let him in.

She grabbed hold of his shirt and kissed him back, just as hard, years of pent-up frustration in her embrace. The desire of a woman heated every inch of her body.

A part of her thought she should slow down.

The rest of her told that part to shut up.

She'd earned this. Who knew when she'd find someone again who made her feel like Devon did?

She kissed him and melted against him. The electric contact of their lips against each other had her panting and flushed. Eager.

Needing.

Devon's hands roamed, touching her in a way she'd forgotten. An exploration of flesh that she reciprocated. She stroked the hard planes of his back through his shirt. Hugged him close, reveling in the intimacy of the embrace.

He cupped her ass and squeezed, yanking her up on tiptoe, giving him deeper access to her mouth the better for his tongue to plunder. It excited her. The tips of her breasts ached, the nipples hard and poking, digging into his rock-hard chest. The hands on her butt angled her hips, grinding her into him, showing her the firm rigidity of his cock, the outline of it clear even with the layers of clothing separating them.

They tumbled onto the bed, landing with a bounce that brought a nervous giggle.

He heard it and paused, his body poised over hers, his expression flushed, his eyes smoldering as he asked, "Are you sure?"

Never surer. Tanya reached for Devon and dragged him down for a kiss that would leave no question. He devoured her mouth, his tongue hot and probing, his lips tugging and suckling.

She made a noise as his lips slid from her lips to her ear, finding the sensitive lobe and making her gasp and writhe under him.

But he didn't stay there long. He moved down her body, his face brushing the fabric of her top, nuzzling her breasts. He pushed up her shirt, still only using his face, the sensuality of it making her mewl in pleasure.

He peeled the garment from her, leaving her clad in only a bra. He sucked her breast through it.

"Oh." It was the only thing she could say as she arched under his caresses. Every part of her was on fire. Aching and needing. He teased her, alternating between her breasts, sucking the nipples through the dampened fabric.

And then he moved lower. His mouth skimmed over her belly, fingers tugging at her pants, yanking them past her hips and down her legs. He stripped them off her, and her panties followed.

He stared at her for a moment, and she had an urge to hide. Not out of fear but shyness. He was only the second man to ever truly gaze upon her nakedness.

"You are so damned beautiful," he murmured before lying between her legs, making her breath catch.

Surely, he wouldn't? She'd never—

"Oh my God." At the first lap of his tongue across her sex, she cried out. How could it feel so good?

Wait, he licked her again, and again, making it feel even better.

She could barely breathe through her excitement. Her fingers dug into the comforter as he feasted on her, spreading her nether lips to lap at her sex. He jabbed her with his tongue, making her crave something bigger and longer.

He flicked at her clit, teasing strokes before he sucked on it and made her come.

She came hard. Her cry strident and raw, the pleasure ripping through her, making her body bow off the bed. He didn't stop. He followed her, his tongue flicking rapidly, drawing out her orgasm, making her cry.

"Enough."

"Not quite," he growled as he grabbed her by the thighs and knelt between them.

Opening eyelids heavy with desire, she saw him pushing at his slacks, releasing his erect cock. Just the thing she needed to truly fulfill the ache inside. Except he paused a little longer to roll a condom over it. At least one of them was thinking because she was past the point of caring.

"Still sure?" he asked, looking adorably sexy.

"Yes."

The tip of him pressed against her moist sex, and she had a moment of trepidation.

What if it didn't fit? What if it was too loose?

What if—?

He slid in slowly and threw back his head and let out a heavy groan. "God, you feel so good."

No, *he* felt good, his thick shaft filling her. Stretching her. The pulsing hardness of it welcome.

But even better was when he began to pump into her, in and out, his strokes diving deep. His cock oh so hard.

He covered her, his heavy body feeling so good, his lips on hers panting and hot. Her sex did its best to cling to his cock, squeezing and fisting it. Each stroke brought a deep shudder. He thrust faster, his body moving in time with hers, his breathing just as ragged as her own, his body flushed.

She came again, her fingers digging into his back, her channel pulsing as she climaxed. Squeezing...

"Tanya. God, yes." He thrust faster into her a few more times before going stiff. She felt the pulse of his cock as he came.

He collapsed to the side but kept them connected, rolling her atop his body, holding her close.

He lazily traced her skin. And wherever he touched, she tingled.

Which seemed impossible given that what she'd just experienced was intense and definitely eye-opening.

Sex with Devon wasn't at all what she'd expected. It was even better. Surely, only because she'd abstained so long. Which might have been why she said... "How long before we can do that again?"

Not long at all.

CHAPTER FIFTEEN

THERE WAS something about waking up beside Tanya that felt awfully nice. Natural, too. She'd managed to stop blushing by the time they got out of the shower, but her skin held a flush from the pleasure he'd given her.

What astonished him was when she said shyly at one point, "Sorry if I'm not very good at this."

Whereupon Devon—who had almost no control left given she stroked him—managed to gasp, "Bunny, if you got any better, I'd be coming before the main event."

Words that made her grow bolder. And, yes, Devon did come before he made it inside her. But that didn't mean she didn't come, too. The taste of her intoxicated.

However, the new day dawned, and she became nervous about getting caught by Cory. Devon respected her enough to ensure that he was wearing pants, but he forwent the shirt for the moment just because he loved catching her staring at him, a dreamy expression in her eyes.

Made a man feel good.

What he didn't enjoy so much was finding out that the hotel restaurant had run into an issue. Mainly, an hour-long wait even to be seated for breakfast.

Tanya groaned. "I should have made a reservation."

"I think you might have been distracted."

"We're going to die of starvation." Her woebegone expression made him laugh.

"How about I go into town and grab us some food?"

"You won't have time. I've got to get Cory to the arena in the next hour." He, at least, was fed. His friend Shane's mom had thought ahead and brought instant oatmeal.

"I'll meet you there. With donuts and coffee."

"Maple cream?" she asked hopefully.

"I promise," he murmured, pulling her against him for a long kiss.

It was only as he pulled away that he noticed the damned envelope. Shit.

He'd been so caught up in Tanya, he'd forgotten all about it. Which just went to show how much he'd changed. Once upon a time, the mission would have come first and damn everything else. Now, he'd rather make a special woman fall for him...as hard as he'd fallen for her.

It might have only been two days since they reconnected, yet he felt something with Tanya that he'd never felt before, not even with his ex-fiancée.

"I can't believe you haven't opened it yet," she said with a shake of her head.

"We can do it now."

"If Antoine is involved in something shady, I'd rather not know."

"Isn't that all the more reason to know?" he retorted.

"I don't need any more reasons to keep him out of Cory's life."

"Could be nothing."

"Then you can check it once you're on your way back with sustenance," she teased. "If you don't hurry, you might miss the game."

"Never. I cannot wait to watch him play. Which means, I better get going." He gave her a hard kiss and then left. Much as he was tempted to stay, he still had to complete his mission, if only to get the paycheck, which he'd need if he were planning to finally call it quits with Bad Boy, Inc.

Might be time to relocate and start over. Show Tanya that he wasn't going anywhere.

He'd just started his drive into town when his phone rang, and he had to pull over to answer it since it wasn't hooked to the Bluetooth of his rental.

"You've reached Devon of Bad Boy, Inc. How can I help you?"

"You can start by not sounding like a happy freak when you answer," grumbled Ben.

"And nice to hear from you, too. Why are you calling?"

"Because it turns out we got our intel wrong. Nothing is going on this weekend that you need to handle."

"What do you mean?" Devon asked, a frown creasing his brow.

"Apparently, the guy running the chop shop scam was found dead in his home this morning. Some domestic dispute between his mistress and his wife."

"I see." Even if he didn't because he'd been so certain that Marcel and Antoine were up to no good.

"You sound disappointed. Harry says not to worry, you'll still be paid for your time. Do you need Sherry to book you a flight home?"

"No. I think I'm going to stick around for a few more days."

"Does this have to do with that thing you've got Mason working on?"

"Maybe."

Ben chuckled. "I hear there's a woman involved."

"Not just any woman. A KM agent."

"Was she after the same target?"

"No, she's at a hockey tournament for her kid."

"How's the kid handling you trying to date his mom?"

"Pretty damned good, actually. We're probably going to hit the slopes together this afternoon after his last game."

"Well, have some fun skiing, you sick fuck. I don't know why anyone would voluntarily subject themselves to freezing temps."

"Says the guy who likes to wear leather pants in hot weather."

Devon hung up with Ben and took a second to ponder. Could it be he'd just wanted Antoine to be a bad guy because it suited his purpose to keep Tanya away from her ex? He was a pretty big asshole if that were the case.

However, he couldn't stem the feeling that there was something off-kilter with the whole Antoine thing. What were the chances that he'd show up at the same arena in that narrow window of time when Tanya would be there?

What of the fact that the guy had a bodyguard who doubled as a crook?

I really should look in that envelope.

He tugged it from his inner coat pocket and stared.

Should he even open it? He'd just found out that Antoine wasn't part of his mission. Could be he'd been spying on an innocent man.

Ha. He didn't believe that for even one second. He slipped out the single sheet of paper inside and immediately started cursing. Shit, shit, shit. This was bad. So bad.

He dialed Tanya as he whipped his car back onto the road, heading for the resort.

Only the call never connected, and he didn't make it back.

Speeding down the two-lane road, he only barely heard the sharp crack of a gun shot. His tire blew, and he went careening off the road, right into a tree!

CHAPTER SIXTEEN

WHEN THERE WAS a knock at the hotel room door, Tanya instantly assumed it was Devon, only to blink in surprise when she saw her son standing there.

"Why didn't you use your key?" she asked, stepping aside to let him in.

"Just making sure I wasn't walking in on something, you know..." His cheeks turned red, and hers surely matched at Cory's less-than-subtle hinting.

"Devon's not here. He went to grab me some breakfast."

"He's bringing more food? Sweet." Cory's eyes lit with delight because, of course, he must be starving. The plight of a growing teenager whose stomach never seemed to get full. The boy could eat anything he liked, in copious amounts, and yet, judging by his slim, athletic frame, he burned it off.

How she envied his youth. "I doubt you'll have time to eat it. We need to get going to the arena."

"If you want, I can grab my stuff and hitch a ride again."

"Why would you do that?"

"Gee, I don't know." He rolled his eyes and snickered.

"Devon can meet us at the arena. I'll text him to let him know. Let's go so I can get a decent parking spot."

"Geez, Mom, I just got here. Can't I at least brush my teeth and stuff?"

"Of course, you can," said the frazzled mother. *What is wrong with me?* Overcompensating because she suddenly felt guilty that she'd been spending more time with Devon than her own kid?

Which made her wonder why Skee was being so nice to her. Surely, he should be showing some kind of resentment. She'd read enough articles to know that children usually resisted their single parent getting involved with someone.

When he emerged from the bathroom, she eyed him. "Can I ask why you seem determined to have me spending time with Devon?"

"He's a cool guy."

Her brows almost rose past her head they went so high. High praise from a teenager. "He is, but I don't think he's the right kind of guy for me."

"Why?" Cory angled his head as he grabbed a clean shirt and undergarments for after the game.

"Well, for one, he doesn't live anywhere near us so it wouldn't really work."

"Or you could start out dating over the 'net or something, see how you get along and if it works out, then he can move."

"You think he should move?" She shook her head. "I doubt he'd do that. He's got a career, just like we've got a life already, and a home. It wouldn't work."

"You mean because it's a little hard, you're giving up." Cory blinked at her. "Hunh. Weird you should say that because all my life, you've taught me if something is difficult, then I should master it. And if I got stuck, you always helped me out." His chin dropped for a second then lifted. "Are you worried I wouldn't give you a hand if things got tough? Would it help if I said I promised to help? I won't let you down."

How had this suddenly turned into her child thinking he'd failed her? "Do you think the fact I don't date is your fault?"

"It is." Said starkly. "You don't date because of me. You don't do anything because of me. Only work."

"I have to work. Need a job to pay the bills," Tanya said with a fake laugh.

"I know you do. But other moms go out and do stuff."

"I go out."

He eyed her. "You go to hockey games with me. Restaurants, with me. Grocery shopping, without me."

He wrinkled his nose. "But you never go to the movies by yourself."

"Because it sucks to go alone." She wasn't about to lie about her reason.

"You have no friends."

That one hurt, and she refuted it. "I have Carla, and—"

Cory interrupted before she finished. "And none of them live close enough for you to see often. You need a boyfriend." Stated with a firmness from her son, who in that moment, spoke as a man.

It drew a laugh. "Did you just seriously order me to find a guy?"

"Yes." His lips quirked. "But only if I like him."

Which could only mean... "You like Devon." The boy had good taste.

But it would never work.

"He's cool. And he talks to me like a person. Doesn't act like I'm a little kid."

"Hey, I might be overprotective, but count yourself lucky. If I had my way, you'd be in a bubble room, protected from everything."

"Mom, that is seriously messed up."

She sighed. "I know. It's hard watching you grow up sometimes."

"I might get bigger, but you'll always be my mom." He reached for her, and they hugged each other tightly, Cory no longer the tiny child she once held in the crook of her arms. "And one more thing," Cory whispered, "get a boyfriend." He snickered and danced out of reach.

"When did you get to be so bossy?" she grumbled as they left the room.

"It's not bossy. Aunt Carla calls it assertive."

Their banter lasted all the way to the arena, making her smile. While Cory went inside to get changed, she tried calling Devon again.

How weird that he wasn't answering. Nor had he shown up. Had something happened to him? Or had he ghosted her?

The moment the thought crossed her mind, she discounted it. Devon's character wouldn't allow him to do such a thing. Which meant he was missing. It took only a few minutes to hack into the cell phone network and trace his phone. It flashed, bopping and reappearing along the highway into town. He wasn't even on his way back yet.

Ugh. It meant Tanya would be breakfasting on arena coffee and a stale muffin. Maybe she'd fancy it up with a chocolate bar.

Entering, she scanned the faces, some familiar, belonging to parents from her son's hockey division. Others bore the look of moms and dads, clutching similar awful cups of coffee.

The arena heaters above the audience seating were working today, their coiled elements glowing an orange-red. She unbuttoned her coat and put her gloves in her lap along with her phone.

Devon's cell phone signal had stopped moving by the middle of the first period. It appeared to be parked at the hospital.

Her heart raced only to slow as the signal moved on. Devon must have stopped in to ask questions. But why didn't he answer his phone?

She tucked her own device away, determined to watch the game instead. It would determine if they made it to the Sunday finals. The team they played against appeared bigger than their boys. The blue uniforms bold slashes on the ice compared to the tamer white jerseys with only stripes of red and black.

As Cory's team dominated on the ice, they took a solid lead by the end of the second period. Three to zero.

The other team was visibly frustrated. They got a little rougher with the boys. Shoves into the boards, testosterone-fueled toe-to-toe standoffs on the ice broken up by the refs. Tanya had been in enough tense situations to see that it wouldn't take much for it to explode.

It happened at the end of the second period. Cory was playing defense and had just taken the puck away from a kid for like the seventh or eighth time.

A hockey stick hit the ice as number five on the other team had a tantrum. The kid went after Cory, only the ref stepped in and ordered him to serve a penalty. That should have been the end of it.

Except at the end of that two minutes, number five

tore out of that box like a locomotive. Tanya stood and could only stare, seeing what was about to happen, unable to stop it.

Still, she screamed, "Heads up!"

Did Cory hear her at all? Because he didn't turn, and number five slammed into him. Cory flew, head-first, into the boards with a crunch. The crowd uttered a heart-sinking, "Oooooh." Then only whispered as no one wanted to be the jerk who sounded insensitive when the kid didn't rise.

No one had better say a word, or she might start shooting. She had to do something to release the panicked pressure building within when Cory continued to just lie there on the ice.

He's okay. He has to be okay. Kids got hit all the time on the ice. Most got up and walked away. She headed down the bleachers, but by the time she reached the bottom, he still hadn't moved.

Despite knowing she could do nothing, she rushed to the glass and palmed it, staring through it. The team trainer was trotting over to her son, his spiked shoes giving him grip on the ice. As the trainer knelt by Cory's side, her son finally lifted a hand. The crowd cheered, and her heart started beating again.

He was alive and awake. She could have sobbed. Cory made it to his knees and swayed. The trainer caught him by the arm and helped him to his feet.

The crowd broke out in applause. No one ever wanted to see a kid injured.

The game resumed with number five tossed for gross misconduct. Despite being upright, Cory wasn't put on the bench. With the trainer guiding, he went straight to the locker room.

Oh, shit. It could only mean they suspected he'd broken something or had a concussion, the latter the most likely scenario given the type of hit he'd taken and how long it took him to respond. Looked like she'd be spending the day at the emergency room getting him checked out.

Tanya headed out of the arena, needing to reach the other side where the locker rooms were situated so she could check on Cory, but upon entering the lobby, someone stood in her way.

"Would you look at that. We meet again," Antoine said, the sight of him unwelcome. There was something slimy about him, fake and condescending.

"I don't have time for this," she muttered.

"You seem upset. That poor child injured on the ice, your boyfriend's child, correct?" Flat eyes waited for her reply.

"Yes." She bit out the single syllable.

"Yet his father isn't here."

"What do you want, Antoine?"

"How old is Cory?"

She lied. "Twelve."

"Doubtful given Midget is for fourteen to fifteen-year-olds."

"They ignored the age because of his size." A lame

lie that Antoine didn't believe for one second, based on the smirk on his lips.

"Where is his father?"

"He had to run an errand." She kept going with the shiny lies, trying to keep him away from the truth. Had to keep him away from Cory.

"Odd how he'd miss his own child's game, but his devoted girlfriend is happy to come in his place."

"Cory's a great kid."

"He is. Such a shame what happened to his father." Said as he pulled an envelope from a jacket pocket.

The words send a chill. "What have you done?"

"Me? Are you sure that's the right question? What about what you've done, Tanya?" He withdrew a sheet, a printout really, with words that she quickly read even though her vision got blurry and her heart began to stutter.

She'd never even thought to hide Cory's original birth records. Antoine was dead. Who would come after him? "How did you get that?"

"Doesn't really matter, does it?" Cory's not-so-dead father waved the sheet in her face. "He's mine."

"Oh no, he's not," she spat. "You wanted to be dead. As far as Cory's concerned, you don't exist, and I plan to keep it that way."

"Harsh, Tanya. So very harsh." Antoine shook his head. "And here I thought we could negotiate in good faith. Why else do you think I'm here?"

"Excuse me?"

His expression held a hint of triumph. "Surely you didn't believe this was a coincidence. I knew you would be here this weekend."

"And thought it best to...what? Accost me? If you wanted to talk, did it ever occur to you to, I don't know, send an email? Maybe give me a call?"

"I could have, but where was the fun in that. Especially since I wasn't entirely sure what I wanted to do until I encountered you again. And saw *my son*." No mistaking the hint of ownership. "It was then I realized I needed to rethink my plan."

"And what was your plan?" she asked through lips frozen with fear.

"I don't think you would have liked it." His lips pulled into a cold smile. "My new plan is a much better one and involves bringing my son home."

"Don't you touch him," she muttered, moving close so the parents nearby wouldn't hear. "I am not the weak and stupid girl you left behind. I will kill you if you touch a hair on Cory's head."

"We both know you're not the violent type," Antoine sneered. "Whereas, I am."

"I might surprise you."

"Doubtful. I already know all there is to know about you, Tanya, miss interior designer. Including that you are still hacking."

The admission only served to bolster her. "Then you know I can ruin you with a few keystrokes."

"I do know, which is why you're going to come work for me."

"Like hell, I will."

"You say that now, but I promise you'll change your mind. After all, we have a common tie binding us."

"Stay away from Cory," she declared hotly.

"Or what?" He offered her a secretive smile. "See you soon, Tanya."

Not if she had anything to say about it.

He walked out the arena front door. She ran to the dressing room, only to find no one there. Someone in the hall sweeping dirt saw her distress.

"If you're looking for the kid, the ambulance just left. Word is they are taking him to the hospital to get checked for a concussion."

The explanation didn't soothe one bit, which might be why she sped all the way to town, passing the tow truck heaving a car onto its deck.

She pulled into the short-term emergency parking and forked over an ungodly amount of money on her credit card before bolting inside.

The emergency room proved to be a chaotic mess. It took her forever to speak to the triage nurse on duty.

"I'm here about my son. Cory Brown."

The nurse never even lifted her gaze. "And you are?"

"His mother."

"Date of birth."

Tanya tapped her foot as she gave out a ton of information only to have the nurse mumble, "He's not here."

"Excuse me?" Tanya shook her head. "You're the only hospital in the area. He has to be here. An ambulance brought him from the arena. Maybe you don't have a name in your system yet. He's the hockey player with the concussion."

"Nope. Next."

Tanya backed away from the window, stunned because now she understood the pit in her stomach. The internal alarm that screamed that her child was in danger.

Antoine took my son.

CHAPTER SEVENTEEN

EMERGING FROM A SMALL ROOM, his head bandaged, the cut on it held together by glue, Devon saw Tanya in the emergency room, her face a terrified mess.

For him? How had she even known that he was in the hospital?

"Bunny," he called, walking only with a slight limp. The blown-out tire had caused him to lose control, and if it weren't for the airbags, he'd have been in even worse shape. As it was, he'd gotten more injured falling out of his car once he unbuckled himself from the rolled vehicle than from the actual crash itself. Sometimes, gravity was a bitch.

"Devon, you're here." Tanya gasped, stepping towards him. "Oh my God, you're injured."

"Did no one give you details? Car accident.

Although, not really an accident. I am fairly certain I was taken out on purpose."

What proved lucky was the fact that the attacker had left right after shooting his tire rather than sticking around to ensure the crash did the job. The diver of a passing car quickly saw Devon's dilemma and called for help. A good thing, because initially, he'd been wavering in and out of consciousness. Damned concussion.

"Who attacked you?" she asked. "Were they alone?"

"No idea. How did you know to come, though? I had no way of calling. I don't know where my phone is."

Confusion marred her brow. "I didn't show up at the hospital because of you. I had no idea you'd been in an accident. I came because of Cory."

Instantly, his focus narrowed, and her frazzled appearance made more sense. "What's wrong with the kid?"

"He got hit from behind in the game. Head-first into the boards."

"Oh, fuck. Is he gonna be okay?"

She shrugged, and her eyes welled with tears. "I don't know. He walked off the ice with his trainer and got taken to the hospital by ambulance. Only, he's not here." She began to babble, emotion raising the pitch of her voice. "They're claiming he never arrived."

The blood in his veins chilled to sluggishness. "They have no idea where he is?"

Her head bobbed. "The nurse said the ambulance crew hasn't come in for over an hour, and this is the only hospital in the area they'd deliver to." Tanya wrung her hands. "He's missing, and it's all my fault. I let Antoine distract me when I should have been with Cory."

"Antoine was at the arena?" Devon asked sharply.

"Yes, and he confronted me about Cory."

"Because he knew." Devon could have groaned. More than ever, he wished he'd been more mission-focused rather than fetching a donut to make Bunny happy. "Antoine's been faking it this whole time," he said, whipping out a few sheets of paper.

"That's Cory's report card. And his picture." She reached for the thumbnail-sized image stapled to it.

"It was in the manila envelope that I found in Antoine's suitcase." The one he'd neglected to open— because he was more focused on her than the job.

Except it turned out that Antoine wasn't part of Devon's job. He was something worse. A threat to Tanya and Cory.

"Geezus," she exclaimed, fists hanging down, pacing in short tight circles. "He knew, Devon. From the first moment we met. This entire thing, the running into him at the arena, the hotel... It wouldn't have been hard to arrange. Cory's hockey schedule is online for anyone to see. I am so stupid." Her haunted expression, ripe with guilt, tore at him.

"How would he have known about you? I thought KM gave their agents new identities."

"Only if it's necessary." Her lips turned down. "In my case, I wasn't running from anyone, so we never saw the need."

He reached out for her. "You couldn't know. The man died fifteen years ago. You and Cory should have been safe."

"Thanks for reminding me he's dead. No one will notice if I kill him a second time." Tanya growled.

"Before we worry about killing him, let's concentrate on finding Cory. Could be Antoine doesn't have him."

The look she shot at him held a deep disdain. "I don't believe in coincidences."

"Neither do I. But we need a plan to get him back."

"How? Antoine's been playing us this entire time. Do you realize we still don't even know what name he's using?"

Devon gripped her chin and forced her to meet his gaze. "Are you giving up?"

Her lips trembled, and her eyes watered, but she managed a weak, "Never."

"Excuse me, Bunny, but I know for a fact you're a lot louder and feistier than that."

"I'm scared," she admitted in a quaver. "He knows what I am, Devon. Knows I still hack."

Which made the situation even more sticky. "So, he's a more knowledgeable asshole than we first imagined. Now we know. Which means, it's time to get angry. We won't let Antoine keep him. Do you have a car here?" he asked, tugging her to the hospital exit.

"Yeah. But where are we going?"

"I don't suppose you have a laptop stashed in your trunk?" He offered her a hopeful gaze.

She scowled. "No. It's at the hotel. I'm only allowed one machine when I travel so I don't look suspicious."

"What do you have in your car then?"

"I've got tear gas in my trunk."

"What else?" he asked, holding out his hands for the keys. She didn't argue and let him take the driver's seat.

"Only some plastic with timers. Lockpicks. Acid strong enough to corrode steel. Two revolvers. Extra ammo."

"Only?" he teased.

"I keep the garrote in the glove box." She leaned forward and pulled out a retractable lanyard with a name badge attached to it. "Strongest stuff around." She extracted the wire and yanked it taut between her hands.

"Brilliant. I've got a pair of small daggers in the soles of my boots."

She glanced at his feet operating the gas and brake.

"Kind of jealous. Women's footwear tends to be slimmer in design. Makes it harder to hide things."

"So, you've got a mini arsenal we can count on, which is good. I couldn't bring much with me on the plane." This was supposed to be a fairly simple job.

"We'll have to hit the resort to use my computer."

"Can you start doing some searches before that on your phone?" he asked, careful not to go over the speed limit. He didn't have his Race the Trap app that fritzed the speed signal on radar guns.

She pulled out her phone. "What am I looking for? Do you know something?"

"*We,*" he emphasized since she'd seemed to have forgotten, "know some*one*. Marcel, who was hired by Antoine."

"Which means his new identity must be someone on their client list." Once she got past the shock, her mind began working in that wonderful way it did. She muttered as she typed. "Let's see if we can find anything on them. Social media. Arrest records. School."

"Now you're on a roll, Bunny. Find some pictures. Anything."

"It's not him," she grumbled a few minutes later.

"Who?"

"Those two clients I pulled earlier. Neither is Antoine." She kept fiddling on her phone.

"What can we try next?"

"I just toxted my office to pull up satellite images.

Maybe we can identify them via cars in the resort parking lot."

Matching them to guests. Good idea. "You think they drove instead of renting?"

"I think it's very possible given we're only an hour's drive from the town I used to live in."

"Shit. Could he have taken Cory to his parents' house?"

"Doubtful. It burned down."

"Is there somewhere else he'd feel safe nearby?"

"Maybe, I don't know."

There was too much they didn't know, but they set out to rectify that once they got to her room. While she ran some kind of computer program to sift all the visible car plates from satellite images and compare them to the names of guests, he put a call into his own office.

Sherry answered. "Bad Boy, Inc., making your real estate dream a reality. How can I direct your call?"

"Sherry, it's me."

"Me who?"

"Me, Devon, dammit."

"Not on this phone you aren't," she sang.

A reminder that the line might not be secure. Given Devon was using Tanya's phone that seemed unlikely. "We've had a situation. Someone took Tanya's kid."

"Oh, no." Sherry sounded appropriately horrified. "You will help her get him back."

189

"Duh. What I need to know is the name of the client who hired me for this job." Because that might make a difference in their next step.

"You know I can't divulge our clients, Devon."

He sighed and rubbed the bridge of his nose. "Yeah, I know, but we're talking about a kid here, Sherry. Possibly abducted by his biological father."

"Cory's dad? But he's dead."

"Not anymore. And given he's not a good guy, and I was supposed to be investigating a bad guy...I'm worried there might be a connection." Because the next step they took would depend on if Antoine knew what Devon was.

"Hold on while I check." He held while Sherry rummaged, not too surprised when she returned to say, "The one who hired us for the job is high up in the government. Quite visible and much too old to be Cory's father."

"Fuck. Okay, thanks."

"I hope you find him soon."

"So do I," he muttered, hanging up. "So, the good news is, Antoine should have no idea who I am."

"How is that good? Nothing about any of this is good." She looked up from her computer to snap, "I walked right into a trap with Antoine. Bad enough he somehow found out about Cory, what I can't figure out is how he knows I'm still hacking. Anyone looking into me would see only a single mom working as an interior designer."

"You said you never changed your name."

She shook her head. "Why bother? Mother only switches identities on those who might be in danger from their past."

"Given your history, it wouldn't be that strange for him to do a search and look for you."

"Why after all this time? And, keep in mind, he didn't contact me directly, he pretended to run into me at the arena."

"Which begs the question, why? Why do it that way? Why not confront you at home?"

"Because this isn't about Cory." She frowned. "But if it's not about him, then why take him?"

"Leverage. He specifically mentioned the fact he knows you still hack, which means he wants something from you, and he wasn't willing to wait."

Her mouth rounded.

"You just thought of something."

"Give me the phone." It was her turn to dial her handler. She hit speakerphone so he could hear the conversation.

A very cultured, womanly voice answered. Marie Cadieux, the most prominent face of Killer Moms. "Darling, how did Cory's game go this morning."

"Like shit. Someone took Cory. I think it was Antoine."

"Excuse me? I thought you just said your dead ex-boyfriend kidnapped Cory."

"He did. Turns out, he's not dead, and he changed

his name. He showed up and confronted me about my son."

"Oh, dear." Mild words that conveyed great depth. "That's not good."

"I know."

"How can I help?" Marie turned businesslike.

"Somehow, he knows I'm hacking. Have we had any strange requests lately? Maybe breach attempts?"

"Dammit, it never occurred to me to flag it." Marie's usual grace gave way to the expletive.

"Flag what?" Devon asked, taking the exit for the hotel.

"We had an issue the day after Christmas. Someone demanded that Tanya meet with him to discuss a job."

"I never meet clients in person," Tanya said.

"Which is what I told this potential client, and he got most irate. Began insisting I give him a way to contact you directly. At which point, I told him we couldn't do business."

"Was it Antoine?"

"I don't know. Give me a moment to load the file." Marie didn't take long to return to them. "The name used on the requests was Marcel Lavoie."

"And the plot thickens," Devon muttered.

"You know who this is?" Marie asked.

"Yeah. We ran into Marcel, too. He's working for Antoine."

"Well, this is a clusterfuck. I'm sorry, Tanya. I

never even suspected they might know the real you. I never spoke directly to anyone. It was all done via the messaging service we use on the dark web. A trace of the send showed it was a security company that filed the request."

"Have we ever worked with them before?"

"No. But I have a feeling they work for someone we have dealt with."

"What makes you say that?" Devon asked.

"Because they asked to meet with the hacker known as Skullgirl," Marie said slowly.

"Shit. Shit. Shit." The expletives from Bunny were shocking but understandable as she went on to rant, "He recognized my goddamned signature."

"Who? Antoine?"

"Yes, Antoine. Remember how I said we met in computer club?"

He nodded.

"We used to hack little stuff together. Grades for kids going to college for extra bucks. The local arena changing announcements for things like Public Swim, to Pubic Hair. And each time we pulled off a hack, we'd leave a calling card."

"Surely, you don't do the same thing on big jobs?"

"Ha, you've obviously not met many hackers," snorted Marie from the phone.

Tanya rolled her shoulders. "Most of the time, we pop in and out, and no one is the wiser. But there are some jobs, big ones, important missions that need to make a statement where we'll drop a flag for everyone to see."

"And you think Antoine saw that symbol, recognized it, and realized it was you."

"It makes the most sense."

"But why go through the trouble of running into you at the tournament? If he knew who you were, then he could have shown up at your door."

"Unless he did, and I was already gone. Don't forget, we left a day early."

"This sounds awfully convoluted."

"We're talking about the same guy who faked his death rather than just leave town."

"So, what's his plan? He must have an end game in sight."

She shrugged. "Steal his son. And, for some reason, make me suffer."

"Again, he could have snatched him from school, and you'd have never known."

"Not reassuring," Tanya snapped.

"I didn't realize you needed your hand held." He arched a brow. "But I will if you want me to."

Once more, her handler reminded her of her presence. "I'll leave you two to figure things out while I poke around some more on my end."

The line went dead, and Tanya sighed.

"It will be okay," Devon promised.

"How can you say that?"

"The same way you didn't give up when your family tossed you out, you'll succeed in this."

"Who told you about my family?"

"You did. Six years ago." During the four-hour stakeout where they'd talked and talked. A moment of bonding that had scared him because, at the time, he'd never shared anything so intimate with even his fiancée. And then he pissed Tanya off by jumping out of a window the next day. It made leaving her to go home much easier.

"You remember me saying that?" She blinked at him in surprise.

It was his turn to smile. "I remember everything you say." Including the way she'd uttered his name when he made her come the night before. "Six years ago, I couldn't do anything about my attraction to you, which is why I pulled that stunt. I wanted you to hate me so I wouldn't care about you."

"And now?" she asked.

"Now, I've got no reason to hold back."

"I'd say we have a big one."

He couldn't help a cocky grin. "You won't be able to use that excuse for long, Bunny. We're going to find Cory. And soon."

"How can you be sure of that?"

"Check your computer."

"Why?"

"Because I think we just got a ping."

Sure enough, the satellite image reverse license

plate search provided a result. It located a rental, paperwork made out to the security firm Marcel worked for. Which in turn led to the company address, which was just a PO Box in Montreal.

"That doesn't help," she grumbled before letting her fingers fly. "There's got to be a real office for this company somewhere."

It became Devon's turn to pace alongside the bed as she muttered under her breath, pulling up random snippets of video with one thing in common, the fact that they all had the same car.

"Can you access its onboard GPS?" he asked. Most newer vehicles had systems that allowed them to be tracked.

"They turned it off."

"You said your hometown is an hour away. Any way of seeing if they went there?"

"I've hacked into the few network-accessible cameras in the area, but nothing so far."

Devon rubbed his chin in thought. "All that trouble, it can't just be for the kid."

"Are you saying Cory's not special enough?" Huffed by an angry mummy bunny.

"That kid is amazing, but I doubt Antoine cares. I think Cory was an accidental byproduct of him wanting to meet you."

"In other words, the hacking job is his real purpose, which means—"

"Antoine isn't done with you. Expect him to call and arrange some kind of a deal."

Waiting, however, wasn't the easiest thing. Tanya did her best to stay busy. Meanwhile, Devon could see her anxiety ramping.

By late afternoon, she was close to exploding. Even hot chocolate couldn't calm her.

Feeling rather helpless himself, Devon did the only thing he could think of. He grabbed her and drew her close for a kiss that left her blinking at him. "What was that for?"

"Being fucking amazing."

"Amazing wouldn't have lost her son."

"We'll find Cory and fix this, Bunny." They had to because the alternative didn't give him someone to kill to bring back her smile.

CHAPTER EIGHTEEN

IT WASN'T until that evening that a bell on her computer went off. However, it wasn't the alarm she expected, hence her frown.

Devon noticed. "What's wrong?"

"That alarm is from the Big Sister spying program I was running. The one sifting for information."

"Guess it hit something."

"I guess." She kept staring out the window.

"Aren't you going to check?"

She shrugged. "Why bother? I know the program works, which will make Mother happy. It doesn't help me find Cory."

"How can you be sure? The last time I delayed on a clue, it cost us realizing Antoine knew everything. What if it's important?"

He had a point. She headed for her laptop and gasped as she read the spot highlighted.

"What is it? What do you see?" He moved to look at her screen. "I don't get it. Looks like gobbledegook to me."

Because he couldn't read the machine language. She, on the other hand, saw a very clear message. She read it aloud. "Remember the house on the hill."

Understandably, Devon frowned. "How is it important?"

"It's a message from Antoine."

"How can you be sure?"

She pointed to the icon embedded in the code. "That was his old signature."

"Do you know what he means by the house on the hill?"

"Yeah." She uttered a heavy sigh. "I know exactly where he's talking about." She spun up a map of a town she'd left and never visited after. She jabbed her finger at the screen. "When we were dating, Antoine told me more than once that he'd be rich enough one day to buy the house on the hill. The biggest one around."

"Holy shit, he went back home? But he's supposed to be dead."

"Why not? It's not like anyone would really remember him."

"Except his family."

"If you mean his adopted mom and dad, they're dead." She'd looked them up a few years ago, feeling guilty about the fact that she'd kept their grandson from them, only to find out that she'd waited too long. They'd died in a housefire.

"He's setting a trap."

"Obviously," she said, putting on her coat.

"You can't be serious about walking into it."

"What choice do I have?" She pursed her lips. "I'll do anything to keep Cory safe."

"Now that we know his location, we'll rescue him instead."

"You think Antoine won't expect that? We cannot go in guns blazing." She shook her head. "I won't take chances with my son's life."

"Maybe you won't take a chance, but can you say the same about Cory?"

The statement made no sense. "What's that supposed to mean?"

"It means, I'm about to mansplain how a guy's brain works. I am a guy." He jabbed his thumb at his chest. "I know how we think."

"Not all guys," she interrupted.

"No, but I do know about the kind of man who wants to do the right thing, who might be scared but loves adrenaline-fueled situations. In Cory's case, not only has he been kidnapped, he's just found out his dad is alive. And that he's not a good guy. He might even have gotten wind that Antoine wants something from his mother. Cory's not the type of kid to allow his mom to get hurt."

As he spoke, Tanya could see where his logic was

leading. "You think he's going to try and escape."

"I'd say that's a given. The question is, will Antoine get pissed when he does? Because that's when it might get real dangerous for the kid."

Men with tempers didn't always hold back their fists. And Antoine had a temper. The rose-colored glasses had fallen off, and she could admit that now. Remember the times he'd lost it, like when a teacher dared to call his parents when he was caught smoking weed in the bathroom. He'd destroyed the man's car. And when Tanya had asked him to stop, the word he'd called her... She'd forgiven him much too easily.

She slammed her laptop shut. "Let's say we decide to go in for a rescue. We don't have time to wait for reinforcements."

"Obviously, and Antoine probably knows that. Just like he knows you won't call the cops. What he doesn't know is that you've got me."

"Um, he knows we're dating."

"But does he know I'm a mercenary for hire?"

Her brow creased. "He shouldn't."

"Of course, he doesn't. Which means, I can be your secret weapon."

"I can't ask you to get involved."

"I insist." He grinned. "Bunny, this is the kind of shit I excel at."

"As I recall, someone always gets shot on your missions."

"Only the bad guys."

"You can't shoot anyone in front of Cory." She wouldn't have her son traumatized.

"Am I allowed to punch people?" The query lilted with hope.

She nodded. "Kicking is okay, too. But try and keep the blood to a minimum. And no choking. Or neck breaking."

"Kind of ruining my plan here," Devon grumbled.

At least he had a plan, because all Tanya had was a voice screaming inside her head, a sound that kept going and going.

Hold on, Skee. Mommy's coming.

CHAPTER NINETEEN

WHEN THE AMBULANCE STOPPED, and the doors opened—not on to the bright lights of a hospital, but that of a lonely stretch of road far away from the arena and even farther from his mom—Cory knew he was in trouble.

Suddenly, all those stories he'd heard of kids being kidnapped sounded all too real, and he couldn't help but recall that few were ever found alive.

The ambulance driver hollered, "Hurry up and dump him before dispatch notices we're stopped."

The guy who'd been riding in the back signaled for him to move. "Come on, kid. Time to get out."

"Why? What do you want with me?"

"We don't want nothing. You should be saying thanks for helping you."

"Helping me do what?"

"Reunite with your dad. Shitty thing your mom did, kidnapping you."

What the heck was this guy talking about? His father was dead.

Cory had no sooner stepped onto the gravel beside the road than a dark sedan slowed to a stop behind them. Heart hammering in his chest, he watched as a guy wearing a suit got out of the backseat and approached him.

Cory looked at the dark hair, the brown eyes, the familiar face of the guy he'd met before in the hotel hallway. A guy he'd not paid much attention to at the time. But with the words of the ambulance attendant ringing in his ears, he looked closely now. Mom had only ever shown him a single picture. A dorky wallet-sized school image of a guy with much longer hair and no smile.

The man in front of him with shorter hair and mature features still didn't smile. But Cory now saw the resemblance. He swallowed hard to hide his fear as he said, "Hey, Dad."

Antoine Legault, a man he had a hard time feeling any kind of paternal attachment to, raised both brows in surprise. "You know who I am?"

"Well, yeah. Mom showed me pictures. Although, it took me a second. You changed your hair."

"And what did your mother say about me?" Antoine asked.

"Said you died too young, and I would have loved

you if you hadn't died." Cory said no more because if he did it might have been along the lines of, "You are a shit father letting my mom be sad all those years."

"Unfortunately, I had to leave. But I'm back now. *Son*." It was if he tested the word. "You need to come with me."

"Why? What do you want with me?"

"What any father wants, a chance to get to know his son."

The words Cory had wanted to hear his whole life. Only now, he wanted to be anywhere but on this lonely stretch of road. "I'm supposed to go to the hospital to get checked out. The paramedics said I might have a concussion."

Antoine waved his hand. "Only because I bribed them when I saw what happened on the ice. You're fine."

Odd, because he didn't feel fine. As a matter of fact, Cory felt quite nauseous.

"My mom will be worried about me."

"Don't worry about Tanya. I'll take care of her."

The ominous words had Cory shivering and casting a glance over his shoulder only to see the ambulance driver slamming the doors to the truck and readying to leave.

He should ask them for help. Except, they were the ones who'd thought nothing of taking a bribe in the first place.

"I really think I should call my mom."

"Not yet. Son." Again, with the odd inflection as if he tasted the word and rolled it on his tongue. "For some reason, your mother wasn't too keen on us meeting."

Probably because his mom smelled shady a mile away.

When Cory was young, he'd often imagined what it would be like to have a dad. The hugs, the playing ball, the rough-housing, the man-to-man talks. Looking at Antoine, Cory didn't get the sense that would have happened.

But he bet it would with Devon. Speaking of Devon, he'd known something was hinky with the bald dude and Antoine right from the start.

"Mom thought you were dead."

"Again, like I said, a necessary thing. And I will explain. Get in the car." His dad indicated the open door.

All of Cory's instincts screamed at him not to. The first rule of the creepy white van if it stopped was don't get in. Everyone knew that.

"I will, but only if you let me call my mom first so she doesn't get worried." And once he saw his mom, he'd have the best argument ever for getting his own phone.

"Ah, but the thing is, *son*, I need her worried. Get. In. The. Car." The firmness of each bitten word got Cory's feet moving even if inside he wasn't planning to comply.

He took a step towards his dad, waited until he started to turn away, then whirled and ran for the woods. He didn't care about the fact that he was hardly dressed for the weather. Running shoes for his feet, and a jacket over his street clothes. No hat. No gloves.

The cold air bit at him even as the hot pants of his breath pushed from his lungs, steaming the air as he stumbled through the snow drifts between the trees. His only hope was to lose Antoine and then circle back to the highway in the hopes that someone would take pity on him and give him a ride.

Only his frantic dashing meant he was vulnerable to pitfalls. The icy crust of snow crunched underfoot, and he sank, dumping cold snow inside his shoe. Worse than that, his leg was trapped!

And it cost him.

A heavy hand clamped down on his shoulder and dug in with fingers of dread. "I got the little fucker," yelled Baldy, yanking him free. He frog-marched Cory back to a glowering Antoine.

"That wasn't a bright idea, son." The words were bitten out. "Get in the car. Now!"

This time, Cory didn't have a choice. Marcel shoved him into the backseat, which bathed him in warmth. However, inside, he shivered.

He'd failed to escape, but he wasn't giving up. He'd get another shot at some point. Maybe not to run away but to get his hands on a phone. It would only take one call to his mom, and he knew she'd come to rescue him.

He'd just have to remember to tell her to bring a gun because he got the feeling she'd need it.

CHAPTER TWENTY

THE HOUSE on the hill didn't look as grand as Tanya recalled. The exterior, comprised of mortared gray brick, looked dirty and worn, the grand two-panel front door not as impressive as others she'd seen.

Yet as a teen, it had seemed like such a wealthy home, the symbol of making it in a world that, at the time, wanted to drag her and Antoine down.

Funny how the things you most admired turned out to not be that great as you got older. Take Antoine for example. Had he always possessed a mean streak? Had she been so desperate to escape her crappy family life that she'd mistaken the scraps he tossed her way for true affection?

She should have known that he played her when he never let her meet his adopted parents. *"They're abusive jerks,"* he'd told her. And she'd commiserated because her parents were jerks, too.

In retrospect, he had said a lot of things that she now found suspect. He always had the right words. Knew how to get her pants off that night she and her dad had had a huge fight. Talked her into giving him her tips from work plus some of her paycheck. The reasons varied each time, usually something about him working on opportunities to get them out of town. None of which had panned out.

Now that she allowed the dam to open, the evidence of his lying piled up. The fact that she never saw the inside of his house. Even in school, he didn't pay her much attention. It was only when they were in private that he made her feel special.

Yet it turned out he'd hidden his true thoughts, his real feelings, and his plans to disappear.

God, I was so stupid. And her friends had tried to tell her. Told her that she was being dumb. Holding on to a memory, making him into something he never was.

I let fear control me. Fear that used Antoine as her shield to muddle through the world, never letting anyone get close except her son.

And what of her sisters? She pursed her lips. Mustn't forget the true family bonds she'd made with sisters from a whole bunch of other misters.

It seemed she'd been caring more than she comprehended. All of which led her to realize, staring at a shabby representation of her past, that it was time to let it go. Like literally bury the actual man holding her back.

But only once Cory was safe. Then she'd make sure Antoine never threatened either of them again.

She showed up at the door alone, wondering just how much he knew. After all, he knew she hired out as a hacker. That didn't mean he knew the rest. Tanya might not participate on missions in the same way as the other KM agents, but she'd received the same training. She could be deadly if she needed to be.

What of Devon? Had Antoine discovered his true abilities?

Devon—the man intent on sticking around and helping—remained convinced that he'd gone undetected. Hopefully, that was the case, because she was counting on Devon to retrieve Cory while she took care of Antoine.

The door opened before she had a chance to raise her fist and knock. The top of Marcel's head showed hints of stubble that enhanced his perpetual glower.

"Where is my son?" she demanded, not in the mood to play nice with this gorilla.

"The little shit is cooling his heels in a bedroom."

The rude name almost had her hurting him. Call her son a little shit? *I don't think so.* But she couldn't show her hand—or skills—yet. "Take me to him."

"Nope. Boss said to take you straight to him. Hands up."

"Excuse me?"

"I'm frisking you, lady. Can't have you smuggling

in a gun and shooting my boss. Also going to be checking you for listening devices."

"Fine," she huffed in annoyance. The thug wouldn't find anything. She'd taken Devon's advice and come unarmed. Let Antoine be lulled into a false sense of security. It would feel all the better when she later slammed his face off something hard.

The hands didn't linger at least, patting her quickly and efficiently before Marcel indicated the interior of the house. "The boss is in his office. This way."

Following slowly, she glanced to her right, noticing a massive dining room, the mahogany wood furniture carved and heavy. To her left, a living room.

Marcel led the way down a hall, which split the house. Wearing only a long-sleeved Henley, his gun was openly visible, strapped to his side. Recalling the incident with Devon outside her room, she already knew he was quick to draw it.

Inside, the house appeared a little less worn and quite grand still, the wooden floors newly varnished yet tired-looking. The walls were freshly painted, but she could see spots in the trim where paint couldn't hide the dents and scuffs of age, the thickness of it sealing the damage to the wall.

The hall had a door tucked under the stairs to the second floor, another at the far end, but Marcel took her left through a doorway that spilled into a library, the shelves built in and made of dark, varnished wood, most of them empty and dusty. There was no other furniture. No Antoine either.

Marcel strode to the French doors through which spilled some light, the frosted panes hiding whatever lay past them. He flung them open, and she got her first peek at the office situated in a glass atrium at the back of the house, what many often called a three-season room. Even with a fire roaring in the stone fireplace, there was a chill in the air, and the glass fogged, making it impossible to see outside.

Antoine stood alone in the room, hands tucked behind his back, pretending to look elsewhere, obviously intending to make her feel at a disadvantage. Despite his nice suit and even his pleasant features, she hated him. The man had no integrity.

"She came alone," Marcel announced.

Tanya bit her lip rather than smirk at how wrong he was. Perhaps this would work, after all.

Turning, Antoine held her gaze as he said, "Thank you, Marcel. You may leave."

She didn't wait for the guard to close the doors behind him before she launched into a tightly controlled rant. "I don't know what game you think you're playing, but it's not happening. I want my son, and I want him now." She doubted simple words would work and yet faced with Antoine's smugness, she couldn't hold them inside.

He didn't immediately reply. Instead, he perused

her slowly, up and down. "Your features are still the same, and yet there is something different about you."

She didn't like that he'd noticed while at the same time reveling in it. Her chin angled upward. "It's called having a spine and no longer being stupid enough to fall for anything you say."

"Yes, you were quite gullible. But passionate. I will give you that. I've fond recollections of the time we spent together fucking."

She almost winced at the crude word. "If I was so dumb, then why bother with me?"

He shrugged. "You were attractive if boring. You were a way to pass the time. I must admit, I'm surprised you ever left our hometown. I assumed you'd marry and pop out a few babies."

"I didn't have a choice but to move on when my parents tossed me out."

"How Christian of them." There was no sympathy in his expression. How wrong she'd been all these years. Stupid, too. To think she'd been mourning something that had never existed.

"What do you want?"

"What any father wants. To spend time with my son. He was quite overjoyed to discover his dear father was actually alive. Less impressed to hear you intentionally kept us apart."

"What?" Her lips parted on a gasp. "You lied to him."

Antoine shrugged. "I don't know if I'd call it a lie so

much as a different version of the truth."

"I never intentionally kept you apart. You were dead."

"And now I'm not, so let me ask, did you tell my son I was alive after our first meeting?"

She sealed her lips.

"Exactly as I thought." Antoine smirked, and her hand itched with a need to slap it.

"You took me by surprise. I was thinking of a way to break it to him that his father is a lying douchebag who should have remained dead."

Antoine grabbed at his chest over his heart. "You wound me."

"I highly doubt it."

"Do not pretend to be so high and mighty," he said with a sneer. "You are no better than I am. You had no intention of ever telling Cory. Just like you planned to keep it a secret from me."

Which, when said aloud, sounded bad until she remembered the crucial part. "That doesn't give you the right to kidnap my son."

"It's not kidnapping if we're related."

"Actually, it is. Give me back my son."

"No."

She pursed her lips. "You are unbelievable. What is this really about? You can't tell me it's because you want to spend time with Cory." The man before her didn't have the emotional capacity to be a father.

"He's mine, and I'm claiming him."

Her brows rose as high as they could go. "He is not a possession. And I'll tell you right now, that if you want custody, you'd better be ready to take me to court. Let's see what a judge has to say about your actions."

Once more, Antoine offered a smug smirk. "You obviously mistake me for a person who obeys the law."

No, she hadn't. Because law-abiding folk didn't fake their own deaths.

"Give me my son." Because she was starting to lose patience and she'd yet to hear the signal indicating that Cory was far away. Had Devon failed to infiltrate and find him?

"Aren't you the least bit curious as to how I found out about you and Cory?"

"You hired me."

"Not exactly. My mother did."

The reply made no sense. "Your mother is dead."

"I'm speaking of my biological one." Antoine strode to a photo on the mantel that showed a younger version of himself with a woman. "I found her when I left town. My real mother, loaded to the gills with money, and feeling quite a bit of guilt over the son she gave up."

"You blackmailed her."

He cast her a sharp glance. "What makes you think she wasn't overjoyed to see me?"

"Call it a gut feeling. Why did she give you up for adoption?"

"Her father made her. A religious man who didn't

believe in abortion, and her just a teen. She gave me away and never tried to find me." He scowled.

"It doesn't sound like she had a choice."

"She had a choice. When her father died and left her all his money, she could have looked."

"But she didn't, and so you decided to screw with her."

"She owed me." Said rather ominously. "And instead of repaying me, she betrayed me again. She found out about Cory." His lips twisted. "Knew and changed her will so that if she dies, he inherits bloody everything."

"What?" Tanya blinked at him.

"Fucking cunt double-crossed me. She knew I'd made sure everyone else standing between me and my birthright was dead."

"You killed your family?"

A sneer pulled his lip. "They weren't my family. I have no family because of the cunt. And you're just like her. Trying to keep my son from me." The irrationality of that statement never occurred to him, and it matched the mad glint in his eyes.

"You were dead." As if that mattered. Not in his mind.

"And now, I'm back. Which means, things are going to change. Starting with you. You are going to work for me."

"You've got to be kidding." She blinked at him in confusion as the conversation veered.

"I need your hacking skills."

"I hate to break it to you, but I don't hack anymore. I'm an interior designer."

"Bullshit. I know you're still working at it. I saw your skills firsthand when a hacker broke into a company server a few months ago and caused a certain operation I was in charge of to fail."

It took her a moment before she figured out what he was talking about. "You were part of that money laundering scheme?" A huge case. The owner of the company had hired her to find out who was embezzling funds from within. She frowned. "Your name never came up."

"Antoine never came up," he said smugly. "Nor did my real name, Bertrand Boucher. Others took the fall. But here's what was interesting about the hack. That person left a signature behind. Skull and crossbones with pigtails and a bow. I would have thought you'd outgrown it."

Her lips flattened. "You were the only one who knew I used it."

"I have to say I'm impressed, hawking your skills on the dark web. And for a pretty penny, too. Did you know my mother planned to hire you to steal more of my secrets? She was setting me up for a fall." Antoine shook his head. "Her own son."

"How did she find out about Cory?" Because she'd yet to figure it out.

"By accident, oddly enough. His picture ran in a

newspaper, something about winning some hockey medal, apparently. When I confronted her, she said he was the spitting image of her younger brother. Seeing him, she did some research for shits and giggles." He shook his head.

Tanya's heart sank as she knew exactly which article he spoke of. Last spring, the boys' hockey team had won first place in their division. Their picture was taken and ran in a paper. "Is that why she hired me?"

He laughed. "That was just a big fucking coincidence. It was I who put it together finally. See, I already knew about the hacking, I just couldn't find you. But then I discovered Cory's existence. I am touched you listed me as his father on his birth certificate. It made all the pieces fall into place."

What a symphony of errors. "You should have called me. This wasn't necessary."

"I originally planned to confront you at your home, but when I arrived, you were already gone. Lucky for me, Mother knew where you went. She was the one who originally planned to stay at the lodge for the duration of the tournament."

"What happened to your mother?" Because the way he spoke didn't bode well.

"The same thing that will happen to you if you don't do as you're told."

"I can't fix the fact I exposed your scheme."

"No, but you can get me back some of the money I lost. The men I work with aren't too understanding when circumstances go awry. They expect restitution plus interest for their trouble."

"You want me to steal for you."

"Yes." He didn't try to bend his intent in fancy words. "You will steal, as often and as much as I want, or never see your son again."

Blackmail. She shouldn't have been surprised. "Why do you need me? Why not steal via hack yourself?" Back in the day, they used to bust into databases and websites for fun.

"I stopped playing with code years ago. Management is more my style."

Actually, judging by the things he'd said, being a raving lunatic was his calling in life. Which meant she'd have to humor him because rationality was out of his grasp. "If I cooperate, I want your promise you'll release Cory."

"Separate me from my son?" He grabbed his chest in mock shock. "But we've just reunited. Which is why we'll all be staying together. In this house, as a matter of fact. Just one big, happy family."

The very thought turned Tanya's stomach. "Won't your wife be upset you're bringing another woman home?"

"Ah, yes, poor Isabelle. She shouldn't have had that extra glass of wine at dinner. She never could hold her liquor, and those stairs can be slippery."

Death wasn't new to Tanya. Heaven knew she'd seen it working for KM. What she didn't see as often face-to-face was the depravity of those who truly embraced evil.

If she weren't worried about Cory, she'd grab the pen on his desk and ram it into Antoine's eye. But who knew what Marcel would do if he realized his boss was dead. She wouldn't put it past Antoine at this point to have left orders to kill if she gave him any trouble.

Humor him a while longer. "If I stay here, I want my own room."

"That can be arranged. With a lock on the outside. Wouldn't do for you to try and escape. I should add that any attempt to do so will result in someone losing a finger. You or the boy, I'll let you decide."

"You're sick."

"No, I'm merely in control now. No more women trying to bring me down. You will obey or face the consequences. Is that understood?"

"I understand perfectly well. Now, let me see Cory."

"In due time. First, let's seal the deal." He pushed a laptop across the polished surface of his desk. "In order to give myself breathing room with my partners, I require five million dollars, and you're going to take it from this charity." He pointed his finger at a logo splashed across the website page. No surprise, he'd chosen a non-profit organization meant for children.

As she sat down, Tanya remained aware that she had to stall. She'd yet to hear the signal. Might never hear it. Had Devon failed?

CHAPTER TWENTY-ONE

LUCK DON'T FAIL me now, Devon chanted mentally as he loped away from the main road, moving uphill through thick trees and brush in hopefully the right direction. Tanya had given him a head start before she drove right up the driveway and entered the belly of the beast.

Leaving her without protection remained the part of the plan he liked least, but as she'd pointed out, "*The most important thing is getting Cory out safe. I can handle Antoine.*"

Could she? If it came down to it, would she act against the man she'd once loved, the father of her child?

Devon hoped he didn't have to find out.

Having watched the house for about fifteen minutes before her arrival, he was fairly certain only

Marcel and Antoine were inside. He'd yet to see a sign of anyone else, including Cory.

The need to move quickly meant that he didn't have time to get Mason to bring in a drone and run a heat signature scan on the place. The specialized equipment would have taken a few hours to fly in and then at least another two or three to actually set up. With Cory possibly in danger, they couldn't wait.

It was Mason who'd informed him that Antoine's wife was dead. Once they'd known the house where Antoine wanted to meet, Mason managed to do a property title search and discovered that Antoine was now Bertrand Boucher, son of Gisele Boucher, who happened to be on Marcel's client list.

Fuck.

A widower as of a week ago and, in of a stroke of even more bad luck, his mother had suffered a heart attack and was apparently recovering at home. Devon would wager that all of this had happened around the time Antoine found Tanya and discovered that Cory existed.

A man capable of coldly killing his wife wasn't someone to fuck with.

Armed to the teeth, Devon had only one gun in hand when he darted across the snowy yard from the tree line to the house. This was the part where he couldn't avoid being exposed.

He reached the building and paused, gun held at

the ready, doing his best to hold his breath and listen. No warning shouts, no sound of alarm, just the distinctive noise of a window opening overhead. He hugged the wall and dared to look up. A foot wearing a sock and no shoe dangled. The green ski jacket proved a bold color statement, the actions of the wearer even bolder.

"Cory? What the fuck are you doing?"

"Devon?" The boy glanced down at him in shock, then beamed. "You came for me."

"Of course, I did. Be careful and don't fall, or your mother will kill me."

"I won't fall." Said with the boastfulness of youth. The kid, nimble and quick, made it down to the ground in his socks.

"Where the hell are your shoes?"

"Front hall. They made me take them off before locking me in a room upstairs."

"Fuck. You can't walk through the snow like that."

"I can do it," the kid said bravely.

He could, and would probably lose a few toes to frostbite.

"Front hall, eh?" Devon glanced around. "Follow me and stick close." He edged around the house until they reached a back porch, the wooden slats cleared of snow and faintly lit by an atrium that jutted from the back of the house, the glass panes fogged with heat. Given the illumination, Devon instead eyed the sliding door leading to the deck. Through them, he could see a kitchen table surrounded by chairs. He put his hand on the door handle, hoping it wasn't locked. It slid easily in the track, and warm air rushed out.

"We can't go inside," Cory hissed. "He'll hear us."

"That's a chance we'll have to take. You need shoes. Don't worry. I'm trained to handle this." He offered reassurance but made no mention of Cory's mom. If the kid found out that she was stalling Antoine, there was no predicting what he'd do.

Devon stepped inside, gun in hand, and did a quick check of the kitchen before he beckoned Cory to follow.

"You stay here and wait for me. Do not move," Devon admonished.

To the kid's credit, Cory didn't roll his eyes, just nodded. A smart boy, he tucked himself in a corner not easily seen if someone entered the kitchen.

The room itself, while large, wasn't open to any other spaces. Only two archways led out, through one, Devon could see a dining table and chairs. Gun in hand, Devon crept through the opening leading to a hall. A long corridor with a few doors set in it, all closed. As quietly as he could, wincing when a board creaked under his weight, he made his way to the front door where he could see a boot mat with a pair of bright red shoes sitting on it. Apparently, the teenagers of today were just as keen to avoid winter boots like those of his time.

He made it to the front hall without hearing or seeing anyone, and had shoes in hand, ready to turn around when he heard it. The faint flush of a toilet, then a door opening. He whirled, but it was too late. Marcel gaped at him.

Caught. So, Devon did what he did best. Improvised. "Dude, I can't believe you didn't wash your hands." And he threw the shoes.

The interesting thing about tossing shit at people, even something stupid like footwear? Their first impulse is to duck and cover.

Which meant Devon had a chance to charge Marcel before he realized it was coming. They hit the wall hard, the thud obviously noticeable, but it couldn't be helped.

They grappled, and Devon regretted his decision to not shoot the guy. But knowing Cory was nearby stayed his hand. The kid would probably need counseling as it was, Devon didn't need to make it worse.

Only, it might get a hell of a lot worse given Marcel was tougher than expected.

The slug from a ham fist snapped Devon's head to the side and for a second, he saw stars. Then he blinked and just managed to avoid a second shot.

Note to self: Marcel has hard fists.

A hard head, too, Devon noticed when he finally landed a punch of his own. The dude's head didn't even move.

Fuck it. He had no choice. He still had a grip on the gun in his other hand. He shot, aiming for a leg. He nicked Marcel. But the big guy didn't even flinch, just bellowed as he punched at Devon, knocking the gun from his hand, pummeling him so quick he could only cover his face and upper chest.

The sweep of his ankles sent Devon onto his back with a hard thud. Marcel loomed over him. The one lucky thing? Devon had fallen within reach of his weapon. He rolled to grab it, and Marcel pounced, forcing them to grapple for control.

The bigger guy forced the gun toward Devon's head, aiming it downward, right at his gritted teeth. Marcel knew he was winning, and grinned. "Say bye-bye, asshole."

Klonk.

The vase smashed Marcel upside the head, and his eyes rolled back before he slumped.

On top of Devon.

Cory peered at him from above as he tried to heave the dead weight off Devon.

"Devon, are you okay? Did I kill him?" the poor kid gushed, his voice high and reedy.

Shoving Marcel to the side, Devon could see why the kid asked given the bald man bled profusely. "Scalp wound. Unfortunately, he'll live to be an asshole another day. You on the other hand..." He glowered at Cory. "I thought I told you to stay in the kitchen."

"I heard the fight and had to help."

He could continue to rebuke the kid, but at his age, there was only one thing Devon would have wanted to hear. He clapped a hand on Cory's shoulder. "I'm glad you did. Good job."

"Can we get out of here now?" Cory asked, snaring his shoes and shoving them on his feet.

"Leaving so soon? I would have thought you'd want to stay and get to know your father. Not to mention, why leave when I have your mother?" The cold words weren't as chilling as the sight of Tanya being prodded at gunpoint in front of Antoine.

Fuck. How had shit gone so sideways?

Cory bristled, fists clenched by his side. "You let my mother go."

"Or what?" Antoine mocked. "You're not in a position to do much now are you, *son*."

"You're not my dad," snapped Cory.

"In that, we're agreed. However, until a certain will is changed, you have to live. Which annoys me as much as you."

"Dude, you are one sick bastard," Devon growled.

"You again?" Antoine's lip curled. "You should have chosen a better girlfriend. This one is taken."

"Consider this an official breakup," Tanya said before smashing her head backwards, right into Antoine's face even as her elbow jabbed and she twisted to grab the gun.

In a second, she had it pointed at Antoine while Cory gasped. "Holy shit. That's my mom."

Devon could understand the admiration. What he also saw was how hard she struggled not to end the stream of invectives spilling from Antoine's mouth. Nasty shit Cory listened to wide-eyed.

She couldn't shoot him, not in front of the kid, so Devon did the only thing they could do.

He slugged Antoine in the face. And when that didn't knock him out, he hit him a few more times until it did.

CHAPTER TWENTY-TWO

THEY DIDN'T CALL the cops. Mostly because it would have caused more complications than it was worth. However, the question of what to do with Antoine remained. For the moment, he was tied to a chair and gagged.

As for Marcel? When he regained consciousness and realized that the boss wouldn't be signing any more checks...

"I quit," Marcel stated, face still bloody as he walked out.

Cory gaped. He turned to Tanya and said, "After everything he did, you're just letting him go?"

She grabbed her son's hands. "There isn't much the police can do."

"He kidnapped me!" Cory exclaimed.

"Because your father made up a story about you being kept away from him."

"He's a bad man," Cory insisted.

A glance at Devon meant that a moment of understanding passed between them.

"Why don't we go see if this place has any food?" She steered Cory in the direction of the kitchen, leaving Devon in the front hall.

She could trust him to ensure that Marcel wouldn't be back to cause more trouble. While she waited, she made her son a sandwich from what she found in the fridge. Her phone pinged.

Mother: *What happened? How's Cory?*

Hockey Mom: *He's fine. Eating.* ::emoji of a sandwich and a laughing-crying face::

Soccer Mom: *He better be or I will fly out there and kick some ass.* ::foot emoji followed by the peach one that looked like bum cheeks::

Cougar Mom: *So...are you going to be bringing a plus one to the wedding?*

Tanya stared at the query. Perhaps a little too intently given Devon walked in and said, "What's wrong?"

"Nothing." She shut off the phone, only to frown as she heard a thump overhead. They all peered at the ceiling.

"Is there anyone else here?" Devon asked.

"What if it's my dad?" Cory said, eyes wide with fear.

"Nah, he's still out cold and tied to the chair. I'm going to go check." Devon left them, and Cory resumed nibbling.

"So, is Devon a cop or something?"

"You might say he is special forces."

"Really?" Cory's expression brightened.

"But you can't tell anyone."

"I won't. So, is he going to come visit us now that I know about him?"

"Um. Er." She was saved from replying by Devon bellowing. "Tanya. You need to get your ass upstairs."

Her ass and Cory's, too, since she wasn't about to leave her son alone in this house. Racing up the stairs to the second floor, she headed towards the one door open onto the hall and spilling light. She heard voices.

Entering a bedroom, she saw an older woman lying in bed, her thin arms handcuffed to the headboard.

"Oh, shit," she muttered.

"Mom, language!" Cory teased.

"You're here." The old lady's expression brightened. "Thank goodness you're all right. When Bertrand went crazy, I worried about your safety."

"You must be his mother, Mrs. Boucher." Tanya and Devon moved quickly to the woman's side and began fiddling with the cuffs.

She nodded. "Call me Gisele."

Cory made the connection. "Are you my other grandma?"

Gisele nodded. "I'm sorry we didn't meet before this. I only learned about you a few months ago. I never meant to put any of you in harm's way."

Tanya caught Gisele's gaze and gave a slight shake of her head. No need for Cory to realize just how depraved his father was. He'd already heard and seen too much.

But Cory wasn't about to pussyfoot around the truth. "My dad said you put me in your will as your heir, which made him so mad."

Gisele winced. "He wasn't supposed to know. I'd hoped to keep it secret long enough to finish the case against him."

"What case?" Devon asked, freeing her left hand.

"The one that would put him behind bars permanently." Gisele sighed. "He might be my son, but he's not a good man."

"I know." Cory crept closer and took the frail hand in his. "You don't have to worry. My mom and Devon tied him up."

"It's my fault he turned out the way he is," Gisele claimed sadly. "If I'd only had the strength to tell my father no, perhaps he would have been different."

"Doubtful," Devon muttered just as Tanya freed her right hand.

Tanya agreed but said aloud, "We can't leave him loose. He's too dangerous."

"I agree, but how can we have him arrested? I'm afraid he's already destroyed the evidence I gathered. We have nothing." Gisele shrugged.

"Don't be so sure of that," Devon replied. "I have

friends who specialize in dealing with people like Antoine."

And those people, led by Ben, a senior Bad Boy operative, arrived within two hours in an SUV with tinted windows that took Antoine away, swept the house for weapons and evidence, and then left.

Without Devon.

Tanya found him in the kitchen with Cory, the pair of them wearing chocolatey upper lips, while Gisele watched them, her expression soft

"Did you just feed my son sugar after eleven p.m.?" Tanya asked.

"Yup," they both declared and then giggled.

She rolled her eyes. "You know he's going to be up for hours."

"Yup. Which is cool because it's New Year's Eve, Mom." Cory rolled his eyes.

She'd forgotten, which went to show how hectic the day had been. "I guess we're staying up celebrating."

"Ha. *You* stay up until midnight?" Cory snickered. "Since when?"

He knew her so well. "I can't exactly go to bed and leave you alone," she grumbled.

"I won't be alone. I'm gonna hang with Grandma. If she wants to." Her son cast the woman a shy glance, and Tanya's heart tightened as she could see by his expression that he feared rejection.

Only, Gisele beamed. "I would love nothing more.

Did you know I've seen you play hockey? I snuck out a few times to watch you. You're quite good." They wandered off into the living room, leaving Tanya with Devon. She almost followed.

She wanted to hold her son close and hide him from a world that suddenly appeared more dangerous than before.

Devon neared and grabbed her hand, murmuring, "It's okay."

"No, it's not. I almost lost him tonight."

"Don't kid yourself. That boy is stronger and wilier than you give him credit for."

"I can't believe he was going escape in his socks."

Devon chuckled. "He's going to be just fine. And don't worry about the old lady. She won't lay a finger on him."

"I'm not worried about that. It's the fact Cory knows he's got a grandmother that's the problem." She gnawed her lower lip. "Mother, my handler, won't like this. We're supposed to cut all family ties when we become a part of KM."

"Maybe she'll make an exception."

Or maybe it was time Tanya moved on from there, as well. She didn't need the money. She had enough socked away. But she and Cory could use some family...

She turned from the living room where Cory had disappeared to face Devon. "You never did say what happened to Marcel."

"Yeah, poor guy. Was driving on slippery roads after one too many and hit a tree. Banged his head pretty good. Doesn't remember much of the last few months."

She stared at him. "Did you whammy him with something?"

"Me?" he said, looking horribly guilty. "I might have used a little something cooked up in a lab."

"I'm surprised you let him live."

"Marcel might be a shithead, but he's not really any worse than I am, in a sense. A contract is a contract."

And who were they to judge given the things they'd done for money?

"And Antoine?" she asked.

"About to sing like a canary if he wants to live."

"If he doesn't?"

"He won't be in any position to hurt you or Cory ever again."

She rubbed at her face. "He hasn't asked yet, but he will someday. What am I supposed to tell him?"

"That Antoine went to jail for a long, long time."

That brought a heavy sigh. "Is it wrong to wish he were really dead?"

"I don't, because he was holding you back."

"Fifteen years." She shook her head. "I am such an idiot."

"What's next, Bunny?"

"Heading home in the morning, I guess. Unless Cory wants to stay an extra day. You?"

"Thinking I'll need to head back to the office as well and clear up a few things."

"Of course." She tried to not react too much to his words. What else would he do? Surely, she didn't expect some grand declaration after spending only a few days together. "When are you leaving?"

"The office has got me out on a flight tomorrow morning."

"Oh. Do you need a ride to the airport?"

"I'll be okay, I have to leave rather early, which means we only have a few hours."

"Hours for what?" she asked.

"For me to make sure you don't forget me."

"But Cory..." she said faintly.

"Is fine. And we're wasting valuable time. That bedroom Gisele gave you for the night has a queen-sized bed."

She could think of a half-dozen reasons why saying no was the right thing. But there was an even more overwhelming reason why she should say yes.

Because she wanted Devon. Wanted one more time so she could mark it in her memories. Something good to take away from the mess.

Rather than waste more time, she tugged him in the direction of the stairs and raced him up. Only when the door was shut and locked behind them did she throw herself into his arms, needing and hungry for a kiss. Their lips devoured, and their breaths soon panted.

She had what felt like a lifetime of pleasure to catch up on, and yet only one night.

Clothes fell to the floor, her hands, his hands. It didn't matter who stripped who, only that they were naked. Skin-to-skin.

The friction of his flesh against hers brought a shiver, but she held in the moan, biting her lower lip.

"Are you okay?" he whispered.

"I'm worried about thin walls."

He chuckled. "Good point." He kissed her more slowly, a languorous embrace that caused her knees to buckle. She sat hard on the bed.

He followed, the leaning weight of him placing her flat on her back, his mouth still clinging to hers.

When he reared back to kneel between her legs, she made a soft murmur of protest and lifted heavy lids to see him staring at her. "You are so damned beautiful."

She didn't need him to say it to feel it. It showed in the admiration of his gaze. Slowly, he ran a finger down her body, starting from the hollow at the base of her throat, dipping through the valley between her breasts, then circling them, the sensual caress igniting all of her senses. He rounded them both then dragged farther down over the flat plane of her belly to the curls covering the vee at the top of her thighs.

He then followed the path his finger took with his

mouth, first kissing the pulse beating rapidly in her neck, then scorching a trail down between her breasts. Knowing he retraced the route of his finger meant her breath caught as he circled them slowly, then surprised her by capturing an erect nub. She writhed as he twirled his tongue around the puckered nipple. She arched when he sucked the tip. Sighed when he left one breast for the other, only to change things up by rubbing the edge of his bristled jaw against her flesh.

He stopped his teasing to once more kiss the space between her breasts, his warm breath caressing her skin as he moved downwards once more. Reaching her belly, he paused and nuzzled her navel, tickled with his rough jaw.

She reached out to grab him, reveling in his exploration of her body, enjoying the awakening of her desire and anticipating the pleasurable climax looming ahead.

He finished kissing her tummy and continued his descent, nuzzling her pubes as his body slid farther down. His arms slid under her thighs, partially lifting her, and bringing a quiver between her legs.

Soft kisses butterflied over the inside of her tender thigh.

Teasing.

Feeding her arousal.

Fueling her need.

Reaching the vee of her legs, Devon blew hotly on her sex, and she couldn't help a long, low groan.

"Devon." She whispered his name. "Devon, please."

"God, when you say my name like that..." He buried his face and began to lick her, his mouth hot and welcome on her most intimate place. He slid his tongue between her nether lips, stroking her inside, bringing a deep shudder that had her clutching his hair tightly, enough that he rumbled against her sex.

"Easy, Bunny."

She released him to grab the sheets instead, her hips undulating in time to the movement of his mouth. She bit her lip to hold back the cries of pleasure that threatened to spill, on the edge of climaxing as he continued exploring her with his lips and tongue.

He flicked his tongue against her clit, stroking it back and forth, and she began to quiver, her sex tightening... Needing...

When he inserted a finger into her sex, her channel clamped down tight, and she came. The orgasm rippled through her, and she heard him whispering, "That's it, come for me."

She did. And when he positioned himself over her, the tip of his cock rubbing against her, she welcomed the weight of him. She reached for him and drew him down for a kiss, tasting herself on his lips, not caring.

Her body thrummed with pleasure, and even though she'd come, she was already peaking again. Just knowing how much he wanted her rolled her into a second orgasm the moment he slid into her.

She grabbed for him, digging her fingers into his back, gasping into his mouth as pleasure shook her again. He didn't seem to mind. He kissed her as he thrust, and her hips arched to greet his pumping body.

And when he came, he whispered, "Happy New Year, Bunny."

Indeed, they'd managed to make it past midnight, which only served to remind her how little time she had left. Like Cinderella, she was about to go back to being just a plain old hockey mom.

It meant that she dove on Devon with an intensity that led to a rapid second round, after which she fell asleep in his arms.

In the morning, she woke to find him gone.

I'm alone again. She cried.

CHAPTER TWENTY-THREE

A WEEK LATER...

A knock at the door had Tanya frowning. Cory was sleeping over at his friend Shane's house. It was after eight at night on a Saturday and almost minus twenty degrees Celsius, so it was doubtful it was a salesperson. She went to the door, fetching a gun on the way.

"Who is it?" she asked through the thick portal.

"Me."

The single syllable had her heart racing. Tanya flung open the door and eyed Devon. "What are you doing here?" Because she never expected to see him again.

"I had business in the area."

"Got a mission?" She drank him in, the lean lines of him.

"You might say that. Are you going to invite me in? It's fucking freezing out here."

Bemused, she stepped aside, and he came in, bringing a blast of cold that couldn't stem the hopeful heat burgeoning inside her. "How did you find me?" she asked.

"Cory gave me your address before I left."

"Oh." Then she added, "Cory's not here."

"I know."

She blinked. "How? Have you been spying on me?"

"Nope. Just chatting with the kid."

"Hold on a second, you've been talking to Skee? For how long?"

"Since I left. I would have talked with you, too, but you wouldn't answer my calls."

Because she'd thought there was no point in prolonging the misery. "So, because I wouldn't reply, you decided to hop on a plane and come see me in person?"

"Yeah, and offer myself as a date for your sister Carla's wedding."

"How do you know about it?"

"Cory mentioned something, as did your mother when I talked to her."

"You talked to my mother?" She sounded like a parrot.

"I did. A nice, long chat actually. She mentioned you had room for a plus one."

"The wedding isn't until March."

"Yup."

"It's January."

"I'm a bit early. Which is good. Gives me a chance to get settled in my new job."

Nothing he'd said made sense so far, and that damned spark inside her kept getting brighter. "What new job? I thought you had one back in the States."

"I kind of quit the Bad Boy agency when they wouldn't open up an office in Ottawa. Something about this already being another agency's territory."

"You did what?" She gaped.

"Lucky for me, I found employment rather quickly. It was my apartment that took a bit longer than expected to pack up."

"Back up a second, where are you working?"

"You're looking at the new Real Estate branch of KM Realty and Design."

"But you're not a mother," she sputtered.

"No, but I am madly in love with one."

The words quite literally stole her breath.

He grabbed her hands. "I know we barely know each other, but I want to. Get to know you, that is. And I've already got Cory's permission to date you, for real this time. So, what do you say, Tanya Brown, code name Hockey Mom, sexiest bunny I've ever met, will you be my girlfriend?"

Did he hear the yes in her kiss?

EPILOGUE

ON VALENTINE'S DAY, for the first time since she was a teenager, Tanya had a date. Two of them, actually. The men she loved most in the world took her to dinner and then proceeded to male bond over shrimp then groan over steak, cracking jokes like the greatest of friends.

Best meal ever.

As was the superhero movie they saw after.

But the true present came that night in bed when Devon rolled out of it naked, his body something beautiful to behold. She could have stared at him forever, but he had other plans.

He pulled out a box from the dresser drawer she'd given him to store his things in when he stayed over. A small box.

She sat up.

Oh, no. He wasn't.

He was.

He knelt beside the bed. A man with tousled hair and beautiful eyes.

"Just so you know, I asked for Cory's permission first."

"What did he say?"

Devon smiled. "He said 'I can't wait for you to be my dad.'"

Her eyes teared up. "Oh, Devon."

"Hold on, Bunny, I got a speech ready. Meeting you was the best moment of my life. I didn't know I was missing something until you came into it. You and Cory. I know I might not be the most responsible guy, but I am trying to be better about rushing in. I promise that I will always put you and Cory first. In everything I do. I will protect you with my life. And love your sweet ass forever. So, Tanya Bunny Brown, will you do me the honor of becoming my wife?"

Tears rolled down her cheeks as she held out her hand, nodding her head. "Yes. Oh, yes. Yes. Yes!" She cried happily as he slid the ring on. "But there's just one thing. You know how you promised to always put Cory and me first? Well, think you can expand that to include another?" She grabbed his hand and placed it on her belly.

His eyes widened. "For real?"

She nodded.

He whooped and gave her a hard kiss. Then grabbed his pants and yanked them on.

"Where are you going?"

She thought she'd die of pure happiness when he said, "I gotta tell Cory he's gonna be a big brother, and I'm gonna be his dad."

Which resulted in more whooping. And then ice cream—without the pickles Cory kept offering.

MARCH.

Meredith chose to hit the beach after a day spent making sure everything would run perfectly for Carla's upcoming destination wedding.

The fact that the woman had decided to get married at all proved a surprise, but her choice of doing it on a beach? That took coordinating.

As part of her gift, Meredith had offered to help. Hence why she was here a week before everyone else, talking to the staff, double-checking the details, scouting out a spot where a sniper could take out a target.

Because this Cougar Mom had a job to do in paradise, and no matter how good-looking her target appeared, she had to stay on task.

She went over her plans as she went for an evening swim, the warm water soothing her body. A pleasure after a hot day. Especially since she didn't dare go for a dip when the sun rode high in the sky. A natural redhead, she burned a lovely shade of lobster.

Nighttime was when she got to do the things others did in the Caribbean. Like swimming in the ocean.

Problem being, she wasn't exactly visible, which meant when the Sea-Doo came out of nowhere and clipped her....

She blinked open her eyes and noticed filmy white curtains all around.

Where am I?

A face leaned over her, tanned and handsome, concern in his eyes. "You're awake. How do you feel?"

Horny? Hmm. Maybe not the best thing to admit aloud. Not to a stranger at any rate. "Who are you?" she asked. Only to frown. "Who am I?"

Are you ready for another exciting story, this time about an older heroine? *Cougar Mom* is coming next.